5/13

Mineral County Public Library
PO Box 1390
Hawthorne, NV 89415

D1021563

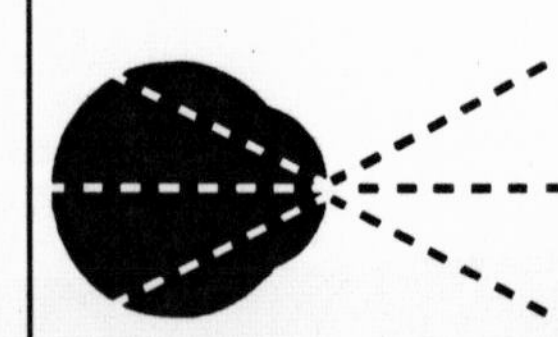

This Large Print Book carries the Seal of Approval of N.A.V.H.

# Brand of Evil

Lee E. Wells

**WHEELER PUBLISHING**
*A part of Gale, Cengage Learning*

GALE
CENGAGE Learning®

Detroit • New York • San Francisco • New Haven, Conn • Waterville, Maine • London

Copyright © 1964 by Lee E. Wells.
Wheeler Publishing, a part of Gale, Cengage Learning.

**ALL RIGHTS RESERVED**
Wheeler Publishing Large Print Western.
The text of this Large Print edition is unabridged.
Other aspects of the book may vary from the original edition.
Set in 16 pt. Plantin.

**LIBRARY OF CONGRESS CATALOGING-IN-PUBLICATION DATA**

Wells, Lee E., 1907–1982.
Brand of evil / by Lee E. Wells.
pages ; cm. — (Wheeler Publishing large print western)
ISBN-13: 978-1-4104-5811-7 (softcover)
ISBN-10: 1-4104-5811-3 (softcover)
1. Large type books. I. Title.
PS3545.E5425B73 2012
813'.54—dc23 2013003466

Published in 2013 by arrangement with Golden West Literary Agency.

Printed in the United States of America
1 2 3 4 5 17 16 15 14 13

# Brand of Evil

# Chapter One

It had been a long and hot ride, angling down south and east from Tucson toward the Mexican border, and Brad Nolan stopped that night, some twenty miles short of his destination, in a sun-blistered little cow town that had no name so far as he could discover. Brad had seen it just at sundown from the top of the pass out of the low hills across the narrow valley, and had changed his mind about making camp. He had been too much alone with too many cynical thoughts and a future suddenly uncertain. To regain some of his old balance, he needed voices, no matter how strange, instead of the lost wail of coyotes over the empty deserts.

It was a lost, little town with a single wide street lined with squat adobe structures, some houses and stores, the inevitable saloon and livery stable, a café of sorts, and a hotel that made Brad decide to camp out after all. But at least he could order a meal instead of cooking it, have a drink or two, listen to news and gossip that might give him a line on the man he was after, Juan Cochran.

Night had descended by the time Brad had ridden across the valley and entered the town. Lamplight glowed here and there, and the dark street seemed deserted. Brad headed toward the bright circle of light the suspended lantern cast over the livery stable door. He dismounted, and the hostler, who had been seated in a chair canted back against the adobe wall, thudded onto his feet and ambled forward.

Brad spoke over his shoulder as he unstrapped his blanket roll. "Off-saddle, feed and water. Stall for the night. Can I wash up?"

"Sure," the hostler said as Brad turned. The man's eyes fell on the badge that reflected light from the high lantern. His eyes narrowed, jumped to the gunbelt and Colt holstered snug against Brad's legs, swept over the tall body, made angular and slightly distorted by the dark shadows.

"Ranger! Don't see many of you down this way."

"Probably not," Brad said shortly.

"Matter of fact, you're the first. Business?"

Brad's long lips moved in a crooked smile and he said dryly, "The scenery — I've never seen anything like it."

"This side of hell." The hostler gathered up the reins. "Staying at the hotel?"

"Would you?"

"Nope."

Brad placed his roll just inside the stable door. "Soon as I eat and have a drink or so, I'll pick this up. And I'd better pay you now in case I leave too early in the morning."

A short time later, Brad ate at the short counter in the café. The owner, a fat man with a sweat-shining bald head, sat near the window, alternately picking his teeth and fanning himself as he covertly eyed Brad's badge. Brad had long ago become used to this combination of awe and curiosity, and paid no attention.

He evaded answering the hinting question the man asked when Brad paid his bill. Brad walked out into the street, thumbed his hat back from his high forehead, and lazily looked around. There was little to see, and the bright light streaming through the batwings attracted him to the saloon across the street.

As Brad expected, he entered a room duplicated a thousand places over the Territory. He thought, with a mental sigh of boredom, that he could have walked to the bar blindfolded without striking any of the half dozen tables between it and the door. Four men stood at the bar, and two of the tables were occupied.

Eyes turned as he entered, fastened with sudden interest on his badge, looked up at him with that instinctive unfounded guilt all men feel in the presence of the law. Brad nodded to no one in particular, murmured his "Howdie," and walked to the bar.

He had his drink, lingered over it, feeling the day's ride slowly wash out of his muscles, and then ordered a second. By then, the little strained silence had long since been broken, though Brad had not been forgotten. Even more than a stranger, he knew, his presence leaned a weight on the room.

The bartender filled his glass, said, "On the house."

"No, I'll pay."

"Damned if you do! County sheriff gets a drink when he rides through, so why shou'n't a Ranger? Man wears a badge deserves a little favor."

Brad shrugged, accepted, lifted the glass in a gesture of thanks, and sipped at it. First time, he thought wryly, the badge has brought anything but wages. He clamped down on the thought, angrily pushed it out of his mind. But he knew it would come again.

One of the men at the bar grew bold. "Heard a lot about you Rangers, but you're the first I ever saw on two legs. Mind if I look at that badge?"

Brad half turned toward him, and the man bent slightly to study the emblem on the faded shirt over the broad chest. He straightened. "Not many of them, is they?"

"Twenty-six."

"To cover the whole Territory! Shuh! Must keep you fellers humping! What you doing down this way?"

"Hank!" the bartender cut in indignantly. "I reckon that's his business and none of ours."

"No secret about it," Brad said easily. "Just riding and looking around in case we'd get called down here someday. Not that we will, but it pays to know something about a country."

"That's real smart of you fellers," the man approved. "Makes me feel the law's looking after all of us down here."

With that, they seemed to approve of Brad if not wholly accept him. The card games went a little faster, and the lazy talk increased. Brad listened to gossip about unknown ranchers and riders, of insignificant incidents that held great importance in this land of vast distances and boredoms.

Then it came. "Heard the sheriff gave up down in Piedra Mala. You can bet Juan Cochran and that mine money are safe below the border."

Brad tried to veil the interest in his eyes as another man spoke from the tables, "I never knowed Blaine to give up like that before."

"What can he do?" another demanded. "There's a million places to hide either side of the border. If Blaine made up a posse, he could figure half or more'd be Juan's friends. You can't breathe without Juan knows about it sooner or later."

"There ain't been a whisper about Juan since."

"Same old way of his — give you a dollar he shows up now Blaine's gone back to the county seat."

"They sure make him at home in Piedra Mala."

"Why not? Half are scared of him and half like him."

Brad became aware that the man at the far end of the bar had been watching him. Brad had caught the swift shift of the man's eyes when Brad had glanced his way. Brad indifferently nursed his drink, looked up, startled, when the bartender said, "Ranger, I bet that's why you're down here!"

Brad caught himself, chuckled. "Not me. Sheriff has to yell for help before we stick our noses in. Nothing like that from your lawman and I hope there isn't."

Their faces fell, conversation died down, and then slowly picked up as the talk turned to other things. Brad finished his drink, signaled his thanks to the bartender, nodded to the others, and strolled out. In the dark street, he threw a look back toward the saloon and wished that he might know more about Juan Cochran. But he did know that Sheriff Blaine had pulled out, as planned, leaving the hunt to the Rangers whom only the Mexican Border could restrict — and not even that if the Rurales were first contacted and agreed.

But Blaine had also expected Cochran to come out of hiding as soon as the sheriff apparently gave up. That was why Brad, on orders, had literally loafed all the way down here, giving the outlaw time to feel secure and, so, a little careless. It looked now, from what Brad had just heard, that Cochran hadn't yet taken the bait.

Brad shrugged slightly and moved on, a tall, lithe shadow that flowed down the dark street. He came to the livery stable, went inside, retrieving his bedroll. The office door stood open and Brad saw, by the indirect light from the dusty street window, the dark shape of the hostler stretched out on a cot. Brad didn't awaken him, but turned out to the street once more.

The bright cone of light fell full on him for a second, and then he moved on into darkness. He found a way along the side of the stable to the rear, walked slowly out from it, and found a bare sandy spot where he could spread blankets. Soon he lay, hands cupped beneath his head, looking up at the bright Arizona stars.

As sleep drifted in, his mind wandered, touching erratically on a hundred and one thoughts, memories, and pictures — the saloon he had just left, vultures yesterday morning, circling dark specks in a clear sky miles and miles away at the head of a barren valley, the glowering face of the outlaw from Oracle when Brad had locked him in the cell at Tucson, Joanie —

He erased her picture instantly, throwing himself over on his shoulder. Mrs. Halstead Miller right now — stop it! he growled mentally. Not that she was a lost love and he was jealous of Hal— but he didn't like to think why she hadn't become Mrs. Brad

Nolan. She'd told him, plain and straight, and thereby set him to wondering about himself and this badge he wore.

The thoughts snapped off as his brain registered a faint sound, unnatural to the night. His hand moved to his holstered gun lying close beside his head. He slid the weapon from the leather, ears strained to the night. He heard it again, closer, the soft thud of a boot.

Brad eased back the blanket and moved silently, crouched, beyond the circle of sand. He turned, waited, gun held ready, and eyes boring into the night. Then a shadow moved against shadows just beyond the blankets he had left. It moved again and Brad eased to his left, to come up behind the skulker.

He stopped, saw a dark shape bending low, and then a voice that barely lifted above a hoarse whisper. "Ranger! Hey, Ranger! Where are you?"

Brad made the edge of the bare spot in two, long and silent, strides. He cocked the gun, deliberately, so that the ratchet of the hammer made a deadly sound in the silence. His voice came low and just as deadly, "Don't move. It'll be your last."

He waited a split second but the shadow remained frozen, exuding fear. Brad moved forward then and said, "I want to see your arms against the sky. Now!"

He eased forward, free hand extended. He touched the man's coat, swiftly patted to his hips and waist seeking a gun. The man wore none, nor was one concealed beneath the coat. Slightly relieved, Brad stepped back. "Strike a match. But move mighty slow and easy."

"No light!"

"Why not?"

"They — someone might've trailed me. Cochran has friends, even here."

"Cochran? What about him?"

"I was in the saloon — down at the end of the bar." Brad had an instant memory of the unshaven, peaked face and the eyes that had secretly studied him. The man continued hastily. "You're after Juan Cochran."

"I say I'm not."

"I don't believe you. Anyway, he's outlaw and you wear a badge. Every lawman I ever heard of's looking for him — and I saw him today — just after noon."

"Where!" Brad blurted

"Less'n fifteen miles from here. There's an old miner's shack in this canyon, and I come on the rim above it, hunting strays. There he was down there. I saw him. His back was to me, but I know Cochran's build and that wild red hair o' his. I ducked back below the ridge, and I swore to God I'd forget it — until you showed up tonight."

Brad kept the gun leveled. "Why change your mind?"

"Cause I figure you come down here for him. Blaine nor the Piedra Mala marshal can't handle Cochran, that's sure. But you could, being a Ranger."

"Thanks for the vote, but if you're so scared of Cochran and any of his friends that might be about, why risk your neck now?"

The man shifted nervously. "I figure you'd not say who told you if I asked. And I've owed Cochran something since he run off my few head of cows four years back and burned my ranch. Just getting started but that half-breed thief ruined everything right then. Now I draw wages. I'd give anyone his hide if I thought I could get away with it. I figure I can with you."

Brad hesitated, then holstered his gun. "How do I find this place?" The man told him. "Can I slip up on it?"

"Not in daylight. That shack sits so Cochran could see a gopher going up or down that canyon. You could gun him down from the ridge, though."

The man eagerly explained how Brad could get to the ridge without being seen.

Too eagerly, Brad thought as he listened, but he said nothing. Finished with the directions, the man demanded, "You'll do it? I've waited a long time to get back at Cochran. He's an outlaw and you're —"

"A Ranger," Brad cut short his babbling. "I'll head out in the morning. . . ."

He watched the man slip away into the darkness, still fearful that some friend of Cochran's would see him talking to the Ranger. Brad stood a long moment after the last faint sounds had died and looked toward the sleeping town, its low squat buildings invisible in the shadows.

This secret visit confirmed what Captain Rollins had said when sending Brad down this way. "Juan Cochran — half Irish, half Mexican, and I guess you can throw in a little Indian. He has friends everywhere, I understand. No point in hiding your badge for you'll be watched wherever you go down there. Every stranger would be. They might be bold enough to set a trap for you, so watch for it."

Brad now rubbed his hand along his jaw. The man who hated Juan Cochran might very well be his friend, and this could be the trap. Brad could have been spotted long before he came to this nameless town, and word sent ahead.

He didn't want to walk into a trap, but he couldn't pass up any long chance to bring in his man. Brad's eyes narrowed as he thought of the informer's eagerness. Brad had said he'd go out in the morning. He glanced up at the timepiece of the stars. Head out now, get there before he'd be expected if this was a trap.

He bent and swept up his blanket and moved silently toward the town and the livery stable. The hostler's snores shook the structure as Brad darted in the wide front doors, risking momentary exposure to the soft cone of lantern light. He found closed doors at the back, opened them, before checking on the sleeping attendant again. The man hadn't moved; the closed office doors, deep slumber, and his snores deadening all sound for him.

Brad led his horse outside, saddled, closed the doors, and led the horse some distance from the line of buildings before he mounted. He sat in the saddle a moment, eyes and ears probing the shadows, but there was no sign that he had been seen or followed. Satisfied, he moved slowly off, cutting toward the road well south of the last adobe buildings. Then he lifted the horse to a faster pace and rode south, reviewing the directions to the canyon where Juan Cochran was supposed to be.

Sometime later, the road lifted to the low pass that had been described, and Brad saw the black humped silhouettes of the hills against the stars. Now he had to slow his pace, and he moved to the right-hand side of the road, literally feeling for the old sign he had been told to watch for. The hills grew higher and pinched in, and Brad began to wonder if he had overshot the road sign in the darkness.

Ten minutes later he came on it, a post badly askew, a rotting board pointing toward the stars instead of toward an abandoned mine somewhere up in those black shadows of the hills. Brad turned off the main road. He threaded a canyon, came out in a wide pocket as he had been told he would. He found another canyon, threaded it, and then another pocket where he turned directly to his left. Just as described, he found another rocky passage, and he halted. His informer had been accurate so far. The old mine shack and Juan Cochran should be about three miles ahead up this black slash of a canyon before him.

Brad urged his horse into the narrow, rocky cut. Within a matter of a few hundred yards, the walls fell back, letting in more faint starlight so that Brad could see the gray substance that marked the rocky, sandy ground. He carefully judged his distance, checking with the directions he had received. The canyon slowly widened again, and he knew he approached the shack.

He reined in and swung from the saddle. Ground-tying his horse, he pulled his rifle from the scabbard, jacked a shell into the chamber, and then walked slowly ahead. Now he could no longer see the walls to either side, and once he almost stumbled over a jumbled stack of thick timbers. They felt smooth and aged to the touch, long abandoned. But they told him he neared the end of this dark trailing. The shack could not be far ahead over to his right in the shadow of the canyon wall, if his informer had been correct.

Brad crouched where he had recovered his balance and tried to pierce the dark shadows over there. He finally moved cautiously out and forward, shifting rifle to his left hand, his right snaking the Colt from its holster.

He saw a darker shape ahead, the shack. He stopped, listening, eyes probing. He half whipped around at a sound to his right, gun leveling. Nothing stirred but the sound came again, that of a horse moving aimlessly. Brad peered ahead, made out the uncertain line of a fence to one side of the shack.

Eyes adjusted now, Brad eased toward the structure, nerves tight as his attention centered on it. Would Cochran be alone? As swiftly as he mentally asked the question, Brad answered it. There was but one horse over in that corral.

He drifted up to the shack, coming at it toward a blind, windowless wall. He crouched at the corner, feeling the rough adobe through the cloth of his shirt at the shoulder. He heard no sound. He edged around the corner and became a flitting shadow to the low, dark doorway.

He flattened himself against the wall beside the frame. Either there was no door or it had been thrown back to admit the warm night breeze. Brad could make out nothing through the Stygian blackness of the interior. He slowly and carefully placed the rifle against the adobe wall, making no sound. It would be useless and encumbering within the shack.

He straightened and edged slowly forward, hand touching the frame. He eased into the doorway, Colt held poised, breath shallow, every muscle tense. He felt the ancient wooden frame on his shoulder and back as he edged into the room, boot toe inching and feeling forward. Dirt floor — his mind flashed — no creaking board to betray him. Now he felt the doorframe on the opposite shoulder, and there had been no alarm. Inside, he would adjust his eyes to the greater darkness, locate a bunk or blanketed figure on the floor, and then make his move.

He swung to flatten his body against the inside wall, eyes straining ahead to the black center of the room. His boot struck something, he sensed a swift movement, and exploding muscles swung him half around.

Something cold and round smashed glancingly against his head, and he felt himself going down.

# Chapter Two

Brad struck the dirt floor, his gun flying out of his hand, his senses spinning. The jar snapped his brain alert, and he rolled toward the wall and his unseen assailant. His body struck booted legs, and his arms wrapped about them. A gun blasted above him, shooting a long lance of red and yellow flame over his head, the thunder deafening him.

Brad's muscles bunched and the unknown toppled over and down, Brad clinging to the legs until he felt the shock of the man's fall. Then he released his hold and threw himself forward, blindly and frantically reaching for the gun that could blast any second. His knee came up in a vicious blow that caught his opponent in the stomach. He heard the man's breath swoosh out as Brad's fingers touched an arm clawed up to the hand and the smooth metal of the Colt.

His opponent tried to twist away, but

Brad's fist struck blindly, connected with a meaty thud in the man's side. Once again Brad's knee came up, niceties in this fight for life against a killer discarded. He connected solidly with the stomach again, as the man twisted away. But it was enough to slam the breath out of his opponent once more, so completely that he could only twist and gasp.

Brad had the man's gun in a second. He rolled away, kicking the body off, and came to his feet. He stood breathing heavily, hearing the tortured gasps and threshing on the floor. Brad clawed a match from his pocket, risked the light by flaming it. He glimpsed a doubled up body and a thatch of red hair. He saw a table, a candle, a twisted blanket in one corner, the metallic glint of his own gun against a far wall. The flame snuffed out.

Brad swiftly struck a match again and lighted the candle. The flame flickered and twisted but gave enough light that Brad saw his opponent still fought for breath. Brad scooped up his own gun, saw a rifle near the blanket. He picked it up, stepped to the door, and threw the weapon out into the darkness.

He turned, leveled his own gun as he shoved the man's Colt into his belt. Now his opponent struggled less, remaining doubled up as he gasped for breath. Finally, he lifted his head, face still strained and mouth open. Brad stood near the table, waiting.

At last the man sat still, staring dully up at Brad as his chest heaved. He made a groping motion with his hands as though seeking support to arise. Suddenly pain-hazed eyes cleared and his head snapped up and his stocky body tensed as though to spring.

"Don't try it, Cochran. No one loses anything by shooting you," Brad warned.

The man's tanned face grew slack in surprise, and his eyes widened and stared at Brad, fastened on the badge. The word burst raggedly from his lips. "Lawman!"

"Ranger," Brad corrected.

Despite the way he held his arms in pain across his stomach, the man on the floor grinned. "Who do you think I am?"

"Juan Cochran."

The man's smile grew wider, and then he laughed, winced, and sat up straight. He pulled his legs under him but froze when Brad made a warning motion with his gun. He shook his head. "Lawman, we've both made a mistake. I thought *you* were Cochran, slipping back here in the night."

Now Brad stared, then fowned, and shook his head. "You fit the description. You were seen from up on the rim by someone who knows you."

The man touched his red hair. "You mean this fits and there ain't anyone in a hundred miles that knows me. The red hair fooled that'n, too, whoever he is."

He indicated his blanket with a move of his head. "Packet of letters over there. Go on, take a look at 'em."

Brad studied him, puzzled and suspicious. "Up against the wall."

The man complied, still grinning. Brad moved to the blanket, risked a searching look. He saw the items that had been rolled up in the blanket and carried under the cantle of the saddle, among them a thin stack of papers, tied with a string. He picked them up and threw them to the man with one flowing motion, gun muzzle never moving from his prisoner. "Untie 'em."

The man complied and pitched them out into the room again. They separated slightly, fanned out on the floor. Brad cautiously picked one up, glanced at the name, "Mr. Orson Mead."

"Me," the man said. "Look at the rest, read the letters. I'm Waco Mead. Heard of me?"

"No," Brad said shortly.

"Bounty hunter. Go ahead, read the stuff. Make sure. I'm getting nervous looking at your gun muzzle."

Brad scooped up the letters, dropped them on the table beside the candle. Everyone directed to Mead, addressed to general delivery in Santa Fe, Phoenix, Tucson. There was a folded reward dodger on a man wanted in New Mexico for bank robbery. The man sitting on the floor against the wall said, "I caught him and the bank paid off. Then I wandered over here and heard about Cochran in Tucson. You can see, the banks want him bad — dead or alive."

"They have — for some time," Brad said shortly.

"Then we're both after the same hombre and the same reward. Satisfied?"

Brad studied the grinning face. "How come you're here?"

"Same reason you are. Heard Cochran holed up in this shack and so I took a look. He was gone but I figured if I was patient enough, he'd return. When I heard you outside, I knew I was right — Juan Cochran's back, but he's gunning for me."

Brad hesitated and then, with a defeated shrug, holstered his gun. The man sat a second, then slowly pulled himself up. Brad looked on a tanned, slightly freckled face, desert-leaned, and angular. Long, thin lips still quirked in a grin, and a bruise began to darken his cheek. Mead gingerly pressed his fingers into his stomach, winced.

"You got a knee like an iron ram, Ranger."

"Sorry."

"Hell! so am I!" Mead gestured beyond the candle. "Fireplace over there. We could both use some coffee."

Soon flames licked greedily at sagebrush and greasewood knots, and a blackened pot burbled on the fire. Now Brad could plainly see signs that this shack had been in constant use. It had not collected the usual debris of an abandoned place, the dirt floor was smooth and hard packed, the small table sturdy and clean.

Mead understood his swift examination. "Juan Cochran's been here, all right. I figure I just missed him."

"And the reward?"

Mead looked sharply at him. "That's the way I make my living."

Brad heard the faint challenge but disregarded it. "I'll bring up my horse and turn him into the corral."

"If you find my rifle, bring it in. I'll close the door, Ranger. Open like that, we're a perfect target against the firelight."

Brad went out, and Mead closed the door behind him. Brad stood a moment, adjusting eyes again to night and starlight, then went to his horse. He led it to the corral, Mead's horse whinnying a welcome. Then he moved briefly about, saw the rifle, scooped it up.

When he entered the room again, he felt as if he walked into a furnace. Mead poured a brown steaming brew into tin cups, returned the pot to the apron of the fireplace. He spoke over his shoulder. "I'm smothering the fire. Mind taking the coffee outside?"

In a moment he joined Brad, who squatted just beyond the door. He accepted the cup Brad held up, and leaned back against the adobe wall of the shack. After a moment, he said, "You don't like my kind?"

"Right now, I'm too tired to know. I rode all day and then we tangled."

Mead chuckled. "Hand it to you — you're a cougar, fast and mean. Hope Cochran's not that bad."

"What you hope to make on him?" Brad asked.

"Considerable — what with rewards here and there."

Brad grunted, surprised. "Heard only the mining company he robbed put up any money."

"I learned to check way back on outlaws," Mead said with a touch of professional pride. "Man gets a price on him one place, generally he's got one somewhere else, especially if he's built a rep like our friend. Cochran's hide — alive or dead — is worth money half a dozen places. Bring him in one place, and the others pay off."

Brad sipped the hot coffee and stared out into the darkness. Mead shifted weight, broke the silence. "Did reward bring you down, Ranger?"

"Assigned — that's all. Man wearing a badge never collects rewards — or seldom ever. They figure it's his job, so why pay him extra?"

"Shame, ain't it?"

"Depends on how you look at it."

"Your side or my side of the badge, it's a shame."

Brad grunted and sipped again. Mead had come too close to wording his own thoughts all these weary miles from Tucson, all those doubts and half decisions. But hearing them from someone else bothered Brad. He changed the subject. "Intend to hang out here?"

"Well . . . not now, since you came. Means Cochran figured he might've been spotted and he moved on."

"Then what?"

"No point in trying to find him — too many places he can hide. So, let him find me. I hear Piedra Mala's always welcome to him so long as the sheriff's not around. So, I'll go there."

"I'm headed there," Brad said.

"Afraid of that, Ranger. That badge of yours. . . ."

"There's not many of us. We're all known."

"So he'll stay hiding."

"He'll have to show up somewhere and sometime."

Mead grinned. "Looks like you and me will waste a lot of time just waiting."

"You get a cougar quicker if you go after him."

Mead didn't answer but moved aimlessly about, now and then taking a pull from his coffee. Brad indifferently watched him. He felt bone tired, and his head ached where Mead's blow had struck, if it hadn't been for his hat, Brad knew he'd have a gashed scalp. Mead made an erratic circle, took a spread-legged stand a few feet away.

"We're both after Juan Cochran. Any reason why we should work apart?"

"Several — offhand."

"One being you don't want to work with a bounty hunter."

"Well, Mead —"

"Call me Waco. It's true, ain't it?"

Brad shrugged. "Something about it, I guess."

Waco Mead pressed, "Because I go for the price on a man's head?"

"For one thing."

Waco snorted. "A damn' poor argument, Ranger! What's wrong with collecting the money someone else offered? I had nothing to do with setting a bounty. But I'd be a fool to pass it up if I put my gunsights on an outlaw. Take Juan Cochran — we're both getting paid for trying to bring him in."

"I am not!"

Waco laughed. "No? You draw Ranger pay every blessed month. Win or lose with Cochran, you get paid. Me, I get nothing and I'm out of pocket if I don't. Now what's the difference except your pay's sure and mine's a gamble?"

Brad stirred uncomfortably. "But to make a living —"

"Where was your last job?"

"Up in Oracle."

"Bringing someone in?"

". . . yes."

"Drew a salary and expenses, too. Now what's the difference between the way we make a living?" Waco reached out a long arm and his finger flicked the badge on Brad's shirt. ". . . except that."

Brad answered uncertainly, "But I'm part of the law."

"So am I, Ranger, in a way. Either of us brings in a man, there's one less killer, thief, or robber running loose. Oh, I admit I make more from the rewards — if I'm lucky. I have been, too. But what's wrong with money?"

"Blood money?"

Waco made an angry sound and then checked himself, answered softly, "Think of that tomorrow when you eat a meal on the Ranger food money."

Brad flung away the dregs of his coffee. He had no argument to bring up, and yet he felt the man was wrong. There was something about that kind of scalp hunting that rubbed Brad against the grain. But how could he explain it? Was a little bit of engraved metal the sole difference, that and the oath of a lawman, be he marshal, sheriff, or Ranger?

Waco cut in on his thoughts. "The outlaw in Oracle — reward out for him?"

"Yes."

"You brought him in. Did you get it?" He waited but Brad's tight silence was answer enough. "Much as you'd make in a year, maybe?"

Brad shifted angrily and Waco smiled in the darkness. "Which of us is the damned fool?"

Brad seathed inwardly at this echo of Joanie, almost her very words and, certainly, her attitude. So, who was the damned fool? he repeated mentally, and suddenly could not sit here any longer. He came to his feet. "I'm turning in. Dog tired."

"Sure, but listen a minute. We both want Juan Cochran. So — let's work together."

Brad half turned away and then slowly turned back. "What's on your mind?"

"We both go to Piedra Mala. You wear a badge, so Juan or his friends will spot you right away. But me, I'm a wandering son going no place in particular. You're in town, say, so Juan watches you. But I'm out hunting. Or I stay in town and you go hunting. Juan moves to keep out of your path and he walks right into me."

"How does that help me?"

"You get your man, Ranger, and take him in. Another good mark on your record and —"

"You get the reward," Brad snapped.

Waco laughed. "That's what riles you! I'm not greedy."

"Meaning?"

Waco sobered. "Working alone and separately, we could both run around in circles down here — or catch a bullet if Juan Cochran had real good luck. We could both lose. This way, we both win by whipsawing that outlaw between us. If you help me catch him, I'll split the reward money."

"Now you're a fool!" Brad growled.

"Not as much as you think, Ranger. I'm saving time, if it works, and there's another reward waiting to be picked up over near Las Cruces."

Brad considered, grunted, "Forget it. I'm not allowed to take side bounty money."

"What's to prevent you? quiet like? There's five thousand dollars offered from here and there for Cochran. I'll slip you two thousand. How many months do you have to work for that?"

Brad grunted again, turned away, and moved slowly toward the shack. Waco called softly after him, "Think it over, Ranger. What could you do with two thousand extra dollars?"

Brad's shoulders flinched but he strode on, jaw set and eyes angry. But he knew that things would have been much different a few weeks ago if he. . . .

With a muffled curse, he rejected the thought.

# Chapter Three

Brad awakened early the next morning, mildly surprised that he had slept so soundly. He had rolled into his blankets across the small room from Waco, his thoughts in a turmoil, Waco's words and offer of reward money bringing them boiling up in his mind. But a brain made dull by sheer physical weariness could not long cope with them and drifted off into a deep, drugged sleep.

Bright morning light seeped around and between the warped planks of the closed door, and Brad heard faint stompings of the horses in the corral. He threw back the blanket, sat up, and his eyes adjusted to the dim interior.

At that moment, Waco Mead stirred, rolled over, and then abruptly sat up himself. He stared dully a second at Brad, and then yawned and stretched long powerful arms above his head. He considered a long spear of golden sunlight lancing through a door crack. “Looks like a good day for hunting, Ranger.”

“Let’s hope it’s lucky for one of us.”

“*Both* of us — if you’ll throw in with me.” He stood up, not waiting for a reply. “Reckon we could do with coffee and breakfast?”

“I’ll throw in on that, anyhow.”

Waco crossed the room and slightly cracked the door. He peered cautiously out and opened the door a bit wider. He looked up toward the canyon rim, searching and probing, finally threw the door wide. “No sign of visitors.”

Brad arose, buckled his gunbelt about his waist, and crossed the room. He looked out on a barren, silent, but sun-flooded world, as yet not stifling with heat. The rocky rim stood sharp and clear against the sky, and Brad gave it only a glance. His horse and Waco’s horse stood with heads over the low corral, ears pricking forward toward him.

Waco came up behind him and, when Brad turned, shoved the small coffee pot at him. “Well out in back. I’ll get the fire going and break out the beans and bacon.”

“I’ve got food in my saddlebags.”

Waco grinned. “You’re visitor, Ranger, even though you sort of barged in. So I do the feeding."

Brad nodded, took the pot, and stepped outside. He found a well between the shack and the canyon wall behind it, noted that windlass, rope, and bucket were in good condition and showed constant use, sure sign that Cochran had used the place as a hideout many times.

Brad filled the water pail and the coffee pot, carried them both back inside the shack. He and Waco washed up as best they could while the fire flamed then settled to a hot glow under pot and frying pan. Brad brought his tin plate, knife, and fork from his saddlebags, and the two men sat cross-legged on the floor near the door. Their eyes constantly searched the canyon rim, the approaches to the cabin as they ate.

Both men took their time over final coffee and cigarettes. Waco directed covert looks at Brad now and then, finally finished his coffee. "What about the deal?"

"It bothers me."

"Why?"

"It's taking money on the side." He lifted a hand as Waco started to answer. "Sure, I know, the rewards are offered. I can't blame you for going after it, in a way. But when a man wears a badge, it's different."

"He's poorer," Waco corrected.

"Because his job is upholding the law and nothing else. If money came first, he'd be just a bounty hunter, trigger happy, thinking of money."

"What else is there?"

"Law — fair trial — jury — the old idea a man has to be proven guilty in open court."

"Reward is pretty fair sign he is."

"Just a sign — and nothing legal. That point doesn't worry you, because it's none of your business. You bring a man in, you get the head money. But me, I'm an officer of the court."

Waco sighed and shook his head. "You take that piece of tin pretty serious — maybe more'n most. Tell you something, Ranger, I have a hunch you'll end up with a big rep as a lawman, if you're not killed first. But I'll also bet you'll end up with little more'n bean money for all the time you wear that badge."

Brad inhaled long and deep on his cigarette, eyes dark and distant on the far, sawtooth canyon rim. He finally sighed. "Yeah, someone else told me that."

Waco shot him a sharp, questioning look but remained silent. Brad inhaled again. "Kept company steady with her a long time. Nothing said, but we — that is, I — thought we'd get married in a couple of years. But

Joanie didn't like . . . this."

He touched his badge. Waco said carefully, "What do you aim to do about it — and her?"

Brad gave a little start. "Her? Nothing. She married a rancher's son. He'll own a fair spread some of these days."

"Kind of break you up?"

Brad made a small grimace. "No — and that surprises me. But I do wonder if I've been a dumb fool and how far I'll get —" He broke off sharp and came to his feet. "Forget it. So long as I wear the badge. . . ."

His voice drifted off and he strode out to the corral, leaving Waco still sitting and looking after him. Brad made a business of saddling up, tightening the cinch, checking it, looking around the rim, but with his mind on something else. Saddled and ready, he half turned and looked toward the shack. Just then Waco came out with his bedroll and came toward the corral with a rolling walk.

When he came up, Brad pulled his hat brim low over his eyes. "Well, thanks for the camp and the chow. Sorry about last night."

"No hard feelings." Waco hesitated, shifting his weight "Ranger —"

"Make it Brad."

"Okay, Brad. You're heading for Piedra

Mala. About fifteen miles, maybe a little more, to decide what to do about Juan Cochran."

"I'm going to find him if I can and bring him in for trial."

"On your own, Brad?"

"On my own."

Waco spat, straightened, and dropped his blanket roll at the corral fence. "I'll wait here a couple hours or so to give you plenty of time to get into town ahead of me, or I might wait clean until sundown. I reckon we're bound to meet at the hotel or saloon, or somewhere in Piedra Mala. Tell me then what you decide."

"You're powerful anxious to give away money. Why?"

"I told you — I can get all the faster to Las Cruces and a bigger reward. Oh, I'll come out ahead, between the two. There's something else," he grinned crookedly. "If you should just happen to be lucky and bring Cochran in without this deal, I'll lose the whole shebang. No, it figures to have you on my side all the way around. See you in Piedra Mala."

Brad's lips flattened. "See you, all right. But don't depend on anything."

"I never did, friend, except what money can buy. Now there's something to tie to."

He glanced at the sun now lifting above the rim and turned back to the shack and its dark, slightly cooler interior. Brad watched him go, then slowly turned to his horse and swung into the saddle. He neck-reined around and rode down the canyon. He looked back over his shoulder to see Waco standing in the doorway. The bounty hunter waved, and, after a second, Brad waved back. Then a twist of the canyon hid shack and man from his sight.

He threaded the series of canyons and small barren valleys and finally came out onto the main north-south road. He turned right and let the horse set its own slow, even pace toward the distant border town.

He came out of the low range of mountains. Ahead, the road sloped down to a sear valley, crossed it, and lifted to another range beyond. His destination should be just over that distant low, sawtoothed range. Brad settled to the saddle, hat pulled low, and broad shoulders slightly hunched against the warming beat of the sun.

He reviewed briefly what he knew or had been told about Juan Cochran. Half Irish and half Mexican, the man already had a long record of shady deals, outright thefts, gunfights, and suspected murders against him on both sides of the border. Cochran, however, had a bold and dashing flair, lacking in the general run of the outlaw. There were stories and hints down in this country that he was something of a Robin Hood, giving most of his stolen loot to the peons.

Brad's lips curled slightly as he recalled the vague stories. Let any man, outlaw or otherwise, give away a few pesos and he became a hero! Understandable, for the people of this barren land on both sides of the border lived always on the edge of grim starvation. Only a hero could be generous as to part with so much as a copper or a slice of bacon, a handful of coffee beans, treat to a fiery slug of cheap tequila. Any of these would be enough to buy loyalty and build the legend.

How much, Brad wondered, of the loot from the mine had Juan doled out — enough to hide him, to buy eyes and ears? But no more, depend on that. Juan Cochran would like and hold money as much as any man, and the mine's strongbox had been filled to the top when the outlaw struck.

A rich haul, but it might be an unlucky, if not deadly one, for the new sheriff down in this county had called for help. Now Brad rode toward Piedra Mala, and he rode with a problem posed by a bounty hunter.

He now came off the slope and onto the

valley floor. The huge bowl seemed to trap, hold, and magnify the increasing heat of the sun. Brad swiped at a trickle of sweat along his cheek, thought of the few hot miles still ahead, and the untold number of them he had ridden the past few years since he had taken the badge.

For what? Wages — little better than a puncher's. A certain pride in his job — but that had added nothing that he could offer anyone else beside himself. It hadn't been enough for Joanie. Not that she mattered, but suppose someone came along who did? He moistened dry lips, growled deep in his throat, and glared at the rutted road ahead, casting the thoughts from his mind.

But he couldn't keep them out. He found himself asking what was wrong with taking Mead's offer? Brad had to find and bring Cochran in anyhow. The identical job, but for wages on his own — for wages and a hefty bonus if he worked with Waco. Either way he brought the man in. So why all this mental riding in circles?

Something wrong — and yet Brad couldn't quite say what it was. Something he felt deep inside that he couldn't quite put into words, a feeling that taking this deal with Waco would be only a first step, the first shadow on his pride.

He approached the lifting slope of the road into the last range of hills. He drew rein, eyes moving along their tops, hardly seeing them as he worked with his problem. He knew that men exchanged favors and many a lawman at that. He had scorned several hints that his silence or a momentary blindness would be to his profit. It was done, not all the time, perhaps, but enough that it was accepted. Why couldn't he? Why hadn't he?

Brad touched the spurs a little too hard. The horse snorted and jumped out and Brad angrily checked its pace, settling it to a steady, easy walk again as the road lifted sharply to the rocky slopes.

He gave full attention to the road, the rocks that could hide Juan Cochran or one of his friends, and so managed to push turmoil out of his mind for a while. The road lifted to a shallow pass, ran briefly through a low canyon, and then opened into the next valley. Far off, hazy in the miles, Brad saw more mountains. They were deep in Mexico and therefore forbidden to him unless the Rurales permitted. However, Cochran could go and come as he pleased. So could any man who did not wear an American law badge, including Waco Mead.

Brad cut that name out of his thoughts

instantly and centered his attention to the sprawling huts, hovels, and buildings that marked Piedra Mala. It sat well out on this plain. Just a mile or so beyond it, Mexico began. The road that dropped sharply down the slope just before Brad became an empty brown slash as it wriggled toward the town.

Brad studied the distant town through narrowed eyes. The buildings were barely distinguishable through heat and distance, but he knew about what he'd encounter there. He'd been in these scabrous border towns before. Over to his right, the range of hills on which he sat curved southward, becoming larger and more complex. The robbed mine would be buried in them somewhere over there.

Brad dashed sweat from his eyes, straightened. He spoke aloud and the horse's ears swiveled back. "Okay, Juan Cochran, let's take care of you. After that I'll decide how much longer I'll work for wages behind a law badge."

He lightly touched spurs to the horse and started down the slope of the hills. He kept his eyes, narrowed against the sun, on the town ahead until he came out on the level and its squat buildings disappeared behind the miles and the gaunt desert growth.

# CHAPTER FOUR

When Brad rode in the north end of Piedra Mala's single street, he had an unobstructed view down its fairly short length. Nothing moved, the hitchracks stood skeleton empty, there was no sign of life. He had the strange feeling that the town had died. Sun blasted down on the low buildings that lined the dusty road on either side. Wooden canopies before the squat stores and buildings threw night-black shadows on the low, scarred wooden porches, creating a false sense of cool shelter. Lanes, rather than streets, wandered off to either side to serve the scattered adobes and ugly frames that were the homes of the townsmen.

The utter stillness seemed unnatural, as though the town waited for Brad, and he had the feeling that secretive eyes intently watched him. His right hand instinctively dropped to his side, close to his bolstered gun. After all, this was Cochran's town.

Brad passed a saddle shop, saw a man just within the open door curiously look up. So, Brad thought, it's not completely a town of the dead. He glimpsed a narrow, but heavily rutted road that meandered off among the distant houses and headed for the hills to the west, probably the way to the mine up there.

A man came out of a general store, halted abruptly in the dark shadow under its canopy, and watched Brad approach. He spoke over his shoulder and another man appeared. Brad gave them a faint nod as he passed but they made no reply, showed no change of expression in faces like tanned unreadable masks.

Brad saw the livery stable, beyond it the two-story hotel next to a saloon. Further on stood a thick, squat adobe, a sign extending out over the low roofed porch. "Marshal," Brad read as he turned to the stable.

As he dismounted, a small, wiry man with a wrinkled, rubbery face appeared in the wide doorway. He had a fringe of white hair about a high, smooth dome, deep tanned as his face. Sun-squinted eyes rested on the badge, held and seemed to slit as Brad aproached, leading his horse.

"Stall and feed?" Brad asked.

The man's eyes jerked up from the badge.

"Sure. How long you staying?"

"Not long."

The man took the reins, looked with critical approval at the rangy bay. "Good animal. I reckon man like you'd have nothing else."

"He'll do," Brad answered shortly, closing any chance for further questioning. He swung saddle roll down after detaching the rifle and its scabbard. "I might be riding in and out a lot."

"Got a stall right up front by the doors."

Brad gave a brief nod and swung away. He stepped out into the street, looked at the hotel, and then swung toward the marshal's office. Behind him, he heard the faint echoing sound of the horse's hoofs on the floor of the stable as the hostler led the animal inside.

Brad continued at an angle across the street. He now saw that the marshal's door and two narrow windows stood open to the street and any chance breeze, but the lawman himself was not in sight. Brad stepped up on the low platform, and his boot heels rapped across the planks.

He looked in the door. A battered desk dominated the boxlike room, beyond which Brad glimpsed cell bars through an inner door. A man sat behind the desk, leaning back in his chair, booted legs up on the desk forming a *V* that framed a long face slashed across with thin lips set now in a harsh line.

The man made no move to arise, merely gave a slight nod as dark eyes coldly sized Brad up. "Looking for me?"

"If you're the marshal."

"I am."

No invitation to come in, no gesture of welcome, only a flat and cold statement. Brad choked down anger, keeping it out of his face. "I'm Brad Nolan, Arizona Ranger."

"Riding through?"

"Assigned here."

"I didn't ask for you."

Brad snapped. "The county sheriff did. Do you have any town law against visitors?"

"Nope. Door's open. Come in if you want."

"I want."

He dropped saddle roll to the floor, carried the rifle with him as he stepped inside. The marshal's eyes followed him as he came up to the desk, leaned his rifle against it. Brad straightened, looked down at the man. "There's generally courtesy among lawmen, Marshal."

The man smiled. "Oh, I got plenty of that, Ranger. Welcome to Piedra Mala. Sorry to see you go."

He pulled his feet from the desk, and his

chair legs hit the floor with a bang. He pulled a stack of dusty dodgers before him and started looking through them. Brad stood a moment, face flushing and his fist doubled.

When he could control his voice, he said, "I didn't ask to be sent here and —"

"I don't want you. I don't need you. This is my town. I'm the elected marshal and I ramrod the law without any help from anybody."

"Did you tell the sheriff that?"

"Damn' right!"

"I suppose he turned right around and rode off?"

The man's lips snapped shut, and anger made a muscle jump in his cheek. Then he grunted and returned to the dodgers. Brad said, "Rangers, my friend, are Territorial Officers. We work where we're assigned with full authority that outweighs yours. I'm working in Piedra Mala, whether it pleases you or not."

The marshal's hand slapped down on the desk. "It sure don't! And in the town limits —"

"I still have authority over yours." Brad eased back and spoke in a more even tone. "I don't want to use it. I'd rather work with you. Now you can make it easy or hard."

"Suppose I make it hard?"

Brad smiled frostily. "Then I'd wonder why and make a report. When it reaches the Governor, he'll wonder why and would send the attorney general down here to find out. I imagine I'd still be here in that case. A marshal can be removed, and I'd be the one to step in if it's ordered."

The marshal sat quite still, eyes ablaze. Then he took a deep breath, moistened his lips. "What do you want me to do?"

Brad smiled and sat down in the chair across from the desk. "I think I know how you feel. I can tell you that neither the sheriff nor the Rangers think you're incapable of holding down your job or running the town. Is that what bothered you?"

The marshal glared, then his eyes shifted, and he shrugged. "How would you feel?"

"Didn't the sheriff tell you he planned to call us in?"

"Well . . . Blaine and me had some words."

"I'm sorry he didn't tell you. Maybe you and me could have started off right."

"Okay, so I reckon it's not your fault," the marshal answered grudgingly. "I'll ride along until you start taking over my job like Blaine did."

"I have no intention of that. I'm interested only in Juan Cochran."

The marshal grinned. "So Blaine ain't lawman enough to handle that!"

Brad answered with a slight edge, "It's a matter of county lines and the Mexican border — like you're limited to the town limits."

"You're after Juan? You're wasting your time. No one catches up with that one."

"That remains to be seen. I'll try. I understand he's often in town."

"Sometimes."

Brad glanced at the marshal's badge on the dark shirt. "Cochran's an outlaw."

"He's done nothing illegal in Piedra Mala, Ranger. Nothing I could arrest him for."

"I see." Brad slowly arose. "Where's Blaine?"

"I heard he got called to the east end of the county on some sort of business. I didn't care enough to find out what. But now that you've come, I suppose he'll be here."

"Might, might not. I'm in charge now, in any case." He picked up the rifle scabbard and walked to the door. "I'll be staying at the hotel."

He picked up his bedroll, gave the marshal a sharp glance. The man had not stirred from behind the desk, black hair and eyes matching the shirt relieved only by the silver of the ornate badge. "If I need you, Ranger,

I'll drop in."

"And if I need you?"

"I reckon you'll find me around somewhere."

Brad grunted and walked away. Deep shade from the low roofs covered him the short distance to the hotel. He stepped out into the sun for an instant and dry-bone dust kicked up from his boots as he walked to the hotel porch. He stopped at the foot of the steps, looked back. The marshal leaned against the door, dark clothing almost blending with the shadows but sharply silhouetted against the brilliant light beyond him.

A few moments later, Brad dropped his load on a bed in a small room that seemed filled to the brim with heat. He pulled up the window sash and felt a slight stir of air through the room to the corridor door that he had left open.

He took a step back and looked out on the street, still empty of life, at the buildings across the way, and then south toward Mexico. Cochran had all the advantage here, Brad thought. A skip and a jump, and the man could be safe across the border. Brad had best write to Tucson and start the process of obtaining official permission to cross himself should a chase demand it.

He turned back into the room, closed the door, and peeled off his clothing, Using tepid water from the huge pitcher on the stand in the room, he washed trail dust from his face and shaved before the wavery mirror. That done, he felt better and dropped onto the bed.

Heat blanketed him but he didn't fight it, having learned long ago that only made it worse. He reviewed his meeting with the marshal and faintly shook his head. He'd get no help there. The man was blind jealous of his small authority.

Brad sighed, arose, feeling a bit rested. He reluctantly dressed again and fled the hotbox room as fast as he could. It was only slightly better in the small lobby. The owner slouched in a chair before the door, fanning himself with a ragged palm leaf. He turned a sweat channeled moonface to Brad as the Ranger came down the stairs.

"Figured you'd be down, even before this. Between now and nightfall you can hardly breathe up there."

Brad dropped into the chair beside the man, mopped his face. "How far's the Golden Eagle Mine?"

"Ten mile south and west up in the hills. You going out there? Juan Cochran, I bet."

Brad admitted the obvious with a nod,

since it would be useless to deny it. The fat man kept the palm leaf moving slowly with a weary patience. "I guess that's about his biggest haul. He'll lay low for a while, especially when he hears you've come to town."

"I've been told he runs pretty open and free around Piedra Mala."

"Well . . . meaning Hank Lewis looks the other way?"

"Who's Hank Lewis?"

"The marshal." The fat man shifted his weight, and seemed to sag deeper into the chair. "Don't blame Hank too much. We're clear down here in one corner of the county, and we don't see a sheriff very often. Juan's got a lot of friends both sides of the border. They wouldn't like something happening to Juan. If Hank went too far, he could catch a bullet or a knife some night."

"How about the sheriff when he comes down here?"

"Oh, Blaine's just in a few days, rides around, and finds nothing. Then he's gone. Juan can scoot below the border or hole up in the hills until Blaine's gone. But Hank's here all the time, you see."

Brad said dryly, "Looks as though there's not much law."

"Oh, but there is! No gunfights, robbery,

or murders here in town. Hank won't allow it and Juan Cochran won't either. Now and then a drunk gets his dander up but cools off in our jail. There might be trouble everywhere else but not in Piedra Mala."

"Sort of a neat agreement," Brad commented.

"It works. We feel safe in town even when Juan and his whole gang rides in. They spend a lot of money, one way or another — at the stores, the saloon, the café. Juan always takes one of my rooms. Quiet a feller as you'd want to have."

Brad glanced at the clock that ticked loudly over the counter in the lobby and pulled himself from the chair. "Near noon. Where's the best place to eat in town?"

"Just one — Mary Alma's. But even if there was a dozen, it'd be the best. Next door."

Brad nodded and walked out on the porch, leaving the fat man to his fanning. Now heat lay thick and enervating on the street and the hills quivered like rocky ghosts in the distance. The café was in the lower floor of a building next door and Brad walked to it, throwing a searching glance north in the direction from which Waco would come. But nothing moved that way except the shimmering heat waves.

When Brad stepped into the café, he stopped short in pleased surprise. The room had a clean, bright look, the walls recently papered, tables placed about, cloths white. The usual counter with its ugly stools was missing. A small bell had tinkled when Brad opened the screen door, and he had no more than taken a step toward one of the tables when a woman appeared in an archway that obviously led to the kitchen.

Again Brad stopped short, caught himself, and swept off his hat. The woman was young, fair skin made whiter by coal black hair that caught little glints of reflected light. Dark brows arched over wide-spaced smoke-violet eyes in which little shadows seemed to lurk. Full lips smiled, but Brad felt that sorrow lurked in the soft folds at the corners of the mouth.

Her voice had a soft throatiness as she spoke. "Hello. Take any table you like." She glanced at the clock high on one wall. "You're a little ahead of the crowd."

Brad nodded, pulled out a chair from the nearest table, and sat down. She came forward, graceful in a high-necked gray dress that flowed smoothly over full breasts. A white apron snugged about her narrow waist over the full skirt that ended just above her toes. Closer now, he suddenly noticed her hands. They were slender, the fingers long, but they showed the marks of constant and hard work.

He realized he stared when he saw a faint red touch her neck, and she said a bit stiffly, "We have pot roast for dinner."

"Fine," he caught his voice.

She walked back through the archway and disappeared. Brad had stared after her. Alone now, he wondered why she had made such an impact. Certainly no other woman had, even Joanie. He shook his head in wonder at himself. What had brought such a beautiful woman to Piedra Mala?

She returned, bearing a heavy plate of steaming food. She placed it before him, left, and returned soon with a thick mug of coffee. She glanced at his badge. "You must be the Ranger they're talking about."

"That's right. I guess words spread fast."

"Little happens here."

"So I've heard, despite Juan Cochran."

Her lips made a brief, faint grimace. "I hope you catch him."

"Thanks. That's the first encouragement I've had. Most figure I won't, even the marshal."

"I know." Her eyes dropped to his badge again. "Arizona Ranger — my husband always said he'd like to be one."

Disappointment and surprise made Brad blurt, "Husband?"

"Dead now. Killed in an accident up in the mine."

"I'm sorry."

Her lovely shoulders lifted, dropped, a silent acceptance of fate, it seemed. She looked beyond Brad to the street. "Here comes Manse Joad from the feed store. We'll be full up now. It's a pleasure to met you, Mr. . . . ?"

"Nolan — Brad Nolan."

"I'm Mrs. Alma."

"I guessed it."

Something in his tone made her eyes sharpen for a second, and then she smiled. "I hope you come back often."

"I will."

Just then the bell tinkled as the screen door opened and Mrs. Alma turned away. "Hello, Manse. Ready to eat?"

"Bet I am, Mary. Guess I beat the rush."

"Just barely."

She turned back to the kitchen. The newcomer moved by Brad, dropped into a chair at a nearby table, and gave Brad a curious, half suspicious look, head bobbing slightly in a reserved greeting. Brad returned the nod and gave his attention to his heaped plate. But he found he listened for faint sounds from the kitchen, for the steps of Mary Alma.

Suddenly, he thought of two thousand dollars and Waco Mead. His fork, bearing a piece of meat, checked just at his lips. Then he hastily took the bite, looked guiltily up as Mary Alma returned with Manse Joad's plate.

# Chapter Five

Joad proved to be but the forerunner of a procession of town merchants who came in during the time Brad lingered over his meal. Each of them cast a swift, sharp glance at him, and then pointedly ignored him, nodding to friends as the tables filled. Brad sensed their withdrawal and, in some cases, wondered if it wasn't covert hostility.

He had long experienced this reserve, and it didn't bother him. He ate steadily, eyes casting about from tanned strange face to face. Some of them would be Cochran's secret friends, he knew, and he wryly wondered how he'd be able to tell friend from foe if it ever came to that. And it might.

Mary Alma moved with efficient grace among the tables, taking orders, returning with the heavy dinner plates. Brad watched her, couldn't help himself. He listened to the musical lift and fall or her voice, liking it. He noticed how swiftly her lips formed to a smile, even though they never fully lost that subtle air of sorrow. The men treated her with easy, friendly respect, and it gave Brad an inkling of her standing in this heat-drenched town.

She brought him more coffee, even before he had thought to ask. He looked up and smiled. It felt suddenly pasted on his lips, for he inadvertently looked deep into the smoke-violet eyes. For a split second he felt he looked into depths of beauty — and something else he couldn't quite define, something almost intimate, as though he had intruded into some personal, secret place.

She made an abrupt, slight move with the cup, and it made a sharp little noise as she placed it before him. She instantly turned and walked away, and he followed the graceful flow of her progress through the tables. The hunter's instinct suddenly made him aware that someone watched him.

He shot a glance to the left. Manse Joad watched, unmoving, jaw suddenly set, lips thinned. Brad read disapproval and anger, and then the man made an elaborate business of eating. Brad could not fully control the slight flush that touched his neck, and the next time the woman entered he didn't once look up. That took an effort.

Brad deliberately lingered a bit over his coffee. Then he stood up, glance swiftly cutting about the room. No one had seemingly paid attention to him, and Joad talked in low, animated tones with his neighbor at the table. Mary Alma appeared in the kitchen doorway, and Brad made a slight gesture that brought her to his table.

He paid his bill, and her smile thanked him. She asked, "Everything was all right?"

"Fine, Ma'am!" He took a slight breath and plunged. "I might be in town a time, and I'd like to come back."

"Thank you." She suddenly smiled, and this time without that touch of sorrow. "Unless you cook for yourself, there's no other place in Piedra Mala."

He grinned himself. "Now that's nice to know — not that I'd care much."

He swung around, sweeping his hat from the chairback and strode toward the door, too much aware of the picture she had formed as she stood so close before him.

The small café had been hot but nothing to compare to the blasting sunlight that struck Brad as he stepped out the door. It took a second to adjust squinting eyes to it, and then the street came in focus. The buildings just across the dusty, rutted way looked shimmeringly unreal, and heat waves looked tangible between himself and the livery stable.

He pulled his hatbrim low and crossed over, unhurried as the heat required. He strode into the black maw of the stable and felt the sun instantly cut off. His horse looked lazily at him from its stall near the door. Brad made a slight grimace of distaste but lifted his saddle from its peg and went to the stall.

A few moments later, he led the horse outside, lifted his foot to the stirrup. He became aware of the marshal, leaning on the doorframe just inside the livery office. The man's brow rose sardonically. "Riding out in this, Ranger? You must take that badge seriously."

"It's part of the job," Brad answered flatly and lowered his booted foot. He caught himself and suggested with distant friendliness, "Want to ride out to the mine with me?"

Hank Lewis pursed his lips in mocking thought, and then slowly shook his head, "I'm just a small town marshal with just enough brains to handle drunks or drifters. Ain't that how you and the sheriff got me branded?"

Brad shook his head. "You wear a badge and that's good enough for me."

"So do you." Lewis straightened and spat to one side. "But it's not good enough for me. Ride your own trail, Ranger."

He hitched at his gunbelt and strode by Brad, every move a mockery. Brad slowly turned to watch after Lewis as he walked lazily across the street to his office and disappeared inside. Brad took a deep breath, once more put his foot to the stirrup, and swung into the saddle.

He neck-reined the horse and, as he moved out, he caught a movement out of the corner of his eye. Lewis had returned to his office door and watched him. Brad rode slowly away, back straight and stiff, though he felt the trickle of sweat between his shoulder blades down to his belt. He turned into the side road that led to the sear mountains. Then he shot a glance back down the street. What with distance and heat waves, he could not be sure Lewis still remained in the doorway.

Brad let his horse set its own slow pace, and it ambled along the hot deep dusty road between a few shacks. It broke out of the town in a few moments and, hatbrim low, Brad peered ahead. The rutted road wriggled like a tortured snake over barren, lifting ground and, some distance ahead, plunged into a pass and was lost.

The whole journey proved to be ten hellish miles through heat, blasting rock, and smothering canyons, little open areas that were only the devil's footprints through these barren mountains. There had been no signposts, but the marks of wide-tread wagon wheels, grooved through dust almost to bedrock, indicated that heavy ore and supply wagons constantly used this route.

At one point the road curved out of the mountains, worked along a wide ledge overlooking the valley below, and then plunged into the mountains again as it turned back on itself. Brad drew rein to rest the horse, removed his hat, and let air touch his sweat-soaked head. His eyes moved down and over the slope, touching on Piedra Mala — now hardly distinguishable from the desert floor — on to those distant hazy blue humps that marked mountains deep in Mexico.

Brad grunted as he thought how easy it must have been to rob the Golden Eagle and cut straight to a haven across the border, even avoiding the town itself. Brad pulled his hatbrim low, gigged the horse, and moved on.

Just as he began to wonder if he had taken the right road after all, it broke out of a canyon onto a high barren plateau. Across the flats, shimmering and wavery, he saw the mine buildings crouched against a far rocky wall. His lips puffed a little sigh of relief, and he moved on.

Approaching the Golden Eagle, he saw the various buildings for processing the raw ore, the black maw of the mine itself boring into the wall of barren rock. A shack held a sign proclaiming "Office" and, to one side, there was a long adobe building resembling a ranch house. Sun glinted from rails that carried ore carts into the mine. He heard a whinny and stomp of hoofs from another long, low building. But that was all to indicate that anything lived.

It puzzled him, this lack of activity, and he frowned as he rode up to a short hitch rail before the office and swung out of the saddle. He mounted the three wooden steps and knocked on the door. No one answered and he turned the knob, to discover the door was locked.

A voice hailed from a distance, "What do you want? We're shut down."

Brad turned toward the direction of the call. He saw a man standing before the adobe ranch house off to one side, a man in white shirt and dark trousers. His features could not be clearly seen from the distance, but Brad instantly noticed an air of assured authority in the stance.

Brad descended the steps. “I’m looking for Dean Harris.”

“I’m Harris. What’s your business?” As Brad turned, the sun glinted from his badge and the truculent voice suddenly softened. “Oh, a lawman. But . . . you’re not Blaine.”

Brad walked the long distance slowly, as though he swam through heat. He didn’t waste effort to reply until he was but a few steps away. “I’m Ranger Brad Nolan, Mr. Harris.”

“Ranger!”

“Didn’t Blaine tell you he’d called us in?”

“Damn it, no! and —” Harris broke off. “Sorry. But you’re here. Come in.”

He stepped aside and waved Brad to the door, a solid, thick plank affair, opening onto inviting cool shadows of the interior. Brad nodded and stepped in, sweeping off his hat, instantly feeling a drop in temperature. The thick adobe walls warded off heat, and he was grateful.

“Sit down,” Harris indicated a comfortable chair. “How about a drink to cut the dust?”

“I could use one,” Brad admitted.

A few moments later, he sipped the whisky and covertly studied the man seated a few feet away. Dean Harris had never been big and Brad sensed that the desert heat had cut him down to muscle, bone, and little else. He had a slightly pointed face, a thin, high-ridged nose. Sun wrinkles made crow's-feet about brown eyes that Brad couldn't quite read. They were both friendly and yet sharp and probing. He had a long, thin mouth, lips moving in a pleasant smile as he talked, but the smile never quite reached the eyes.

He lolled at ease in his chair, drink held in a long and boney hand. His white shirt showed sweat stains along the average chest and under the arms as he moved with a nervous irritability. His voice sounded smooth, modulated, and friendly.

"I can't undertand why Blaine sent for you."

Brad shrugged. "He can only chase Cochran to the county line or the Mexican border. That makes it too easy for Juan. So, if he's to be caught at all, it'd take one of us. I drew the assignment."

"I see." Harris lifted his glass. "Here's to your luck, then. You'll need it."

"So I've heard. But, luck or no, I'll stick it out. The whole border country's pretty tired of Cochran dipping his hand into everyone's money box. It has to be stopped."

Harris reached for the whisky bottle on

the table by his side, gestured to Brad. He poured his own when Brad shook his head and dropped back into the chair again. "Tell me, doesn't the border stop you like it does Blaine?"

"Ordinarily. But the Rurales work with us if we ask. They like law and order, too. They'll be looking for him over there like I will here. Between us. . . ."

Harris noded, smiled approvingly, "Whipsaw!" His face fell. "But it won't work."

"Why not?"

"You don't know Juan."

"I intend to — as fast as I can."

A little silence fell between them that Brad broke after a few moments. "I reckon you'll work with us as well as you did with Blaine."

Harris gave a little start. "Of course! Just tell me what to do."

"First, how did he pull the robbery?"

"Simple enough."

Harris told the story. The mine had closed Friday night, the day before the miners would be paid. The usual two guards had come on duty, and Harris had locked the payroll with the refined ore in the strongroom. Brad interrupted to ask about keys to learn Harris and the superintendent alone carried them. Harris, as usual, had soon ridden off to Piedra Mala.

"It's a hell hole," he said flatly, "but anything's better than this day in and day out. You can talk with someone more than a miner, play some cards, get some news."

He sighed, and then continued, saying Cochran and his bunch must have been waiting for the weekly departure of workers and Harris. The Mexicans always left for their adobes far down the canyon or just over the border. That left the two guards and the shaft superintendent.

Harris shrugged and drained his glass. "They took out one of the guards and then the other."

"How?"

"Pitch night, Ranger. Make a little sound that's not quite right and a guard gets curious. Knock him out when he gets close. Do the same with the other man on the far side of the buildings, and it would be easy to take care of the third man. He didn't even know anything was wrong until a gun barrel slammed against his skull."

"And he had a set of keys?"

"He did. What could have been easier after that?"

"Where was the superintendent?"

"He has an adobe — smaller than this — over near the reduction plant. He was there. He thought one of the guards called him and when he stepped out the door, they had him."

Brad leaned forward, looking out the window, his eyes distant. "Just you and he had keys. How did Cochran know that?"

He caught the faint hesitation in Harris, that split second in which the man seemed to recognize he moved into a dangerous area. It did not show in the man's expression, only in a slight parting of the lips, and then an instant recovery. He strugged eloquently. "Did he have to know it? They found the keys."

"On him?"

"I suppose so. Why do you ask?"

"Just filling in the details."

Harris nodded and then swept up the bottle, stepped to Brad's chair, and filled his glass despite refusal. "Hell, Ranger, relax! I'm not one to stand on ceremony and rules like drinking on the job. You've had a long trip and a tough one. If you figure on catching Cochran, it's going to be even tougher. Drink up."

The drink was poured and Brad made no issue of it. He nodded thanks and sipped at it when Harris dropped into his own chair again. The man drank deep, placed the glass on the table, and slowly rubbed his hands together as he leaned forward.

"Since I called the sheriff in, I've been thinking about this whole business. That payroll and gold is gone for good and ever, depend on it. No one's really to blame, when you come down to it. The guards were tricked, but that happens. The super was knocked out — and that happens. They had an easy way into the strongroom, rifled it, and rode off — to Mexico. And that makes the difference."

"How?"

"It means there's no chance of recovery. Sure, Golden Eagle took a heavy loss, but there's a lot more of that yellow stuff under these hills. More than enough to make up for what we lost."

Brad directly eyed the man. "You take this different than any I've heard before."

"Because I know the chances against us — Blaine, you, and me. All of us have done all we can, maybe excepting you since you just rode in. But I know how it'll go — just as it's gone with every lawman who's tried to catch Cochran. It's like trying to corral a sand devil."

"You're just giving up!"

"Because that's the way it's going to end, anyhow. Besides, my Mex workers are all upset what with Blaine around and asking a lot of questions, looking suspicious. More'n half of them didn't show up until they knew he'd ridden out of Piedra Mala. Now, you come, and I might as well close down the mine until you're gone."

Brad dropped back in his chair with a thud. "You think I'll do that?"

"Sooner or later, and I'd gamble on it. You've had a long ride for nothing. You will have days, or weeks, or months for nothing. In the meantime, I'm half shut down. That's worth money to me, Ranger."

His eyes met Brad's, rested squarely on them a moment, and seemed to speak silently. Brad frowned slightly, and the eyes moved casually away. Harris added softly, "It's worth money — and I wouldn't begrudge it . . . to anyone."

Brad's face revealed none of his thoughts. He carefully placed his empty shot glass on the table beside Harris, stood looking down at him a moment. The man innocently met his stare, and again something unspoken hung in the still air.

Brad hitched at his gunbelt. "You have a problem there."

Harris' shallow face lighted. "That I do!"

"I'll keep it in mind while I look around."

Harris' jaw dropped, and then his cheeks suffered a dull red. Brad said pleasantly, "I guess I've learned all I can this time. Mind if I look around?"

"I —" Harris choked, and added with a snap, "Help yourself."

# Chapter Six

Brad turned on his heel and walked to the door. As he opened it, Harris hastily came to his feet. "If you'll give me time to get my hat, I'll go along."

Brad closed the door and waited while Harris disappeared momentarily into another room. The manager returned, and now all trace of antagonism seemed gone and he came readily forward. The two men plunged into the blasting sunlight, squinted their eyes to adjust, and then Harris led the way.

He retraced Brad's path to the office and stopped before the small structure. He swept his arm about. "You can see just about everything from here."

Brad's eyes followed Harris' pointing finger as he indicated the various structures, the path that led along a narrow canyon to the workers' adobes, out of sight beyond the low hills that bounded that side of the flat. It took but a few moments to see all the Golden Eagle Mine buildings.

"How do you figure Cochran worked the robbery?" Brad asked.

"We know. Sign showed how his bunch drifted down that canyon over there." Harris made a gesture. "The guards always split up on their patrol, keeping on opposite sides of the area. That proved to be a mistake, of course."

Brad, as Harris described the situation, could see how easily the two men could be taken out one at a time. He nodded bleakly as Harris finished, then indicated a smaller adobe. "That's the superintendent's house. Cochran cut across here in the dark, knocked — and you know the rest."

"Where's the strongroom?"

Harris swung around to the office structure. "I'll show you."

He unlocked the door, and Brad followed him inside. He looked on a small general office, consisting of a battered desk and bookkeeper's stand beyond a wooden railing. A smaller office was obviously Harris'. The manager pushed through the swing gate, led the way to another door, and opened it. A short corridor ended before a heavy, solid iron door set deep in thick adobe. Harris pulled keys from his pocket, and opened double locks. He swung the door in on a small black cavern, and struck a match.

Brad saw canvas bags on the floor, a small safe; Harris found a small lamp on a ledge, lit it. He indicated the bags. "You see, we're already making up part of our loss. The payroll money's kept overnight in the safe."

"Locked?"

"Well, no — and that proved to be another mistake. But —" Harris indicated the walls. "This room's sheathed in iron and the cash in here just one night, paid out the next day. And only two of us have keys —"

Brad nodded and turned back into the main office. Harris followed him in a moment, locking the thick metal door. "Anything else?" he asked Brad.

"How about the superintendent?"

"I can show you his place."

"I'd like to talk to him."

"I wish you could, Nolan." Harris' face grew dark. "But there's no chance."

Brad swung around sharply. "Why not?"

"Well, Orin had a bad habit of taking his fun in a cantina across the border — a woman over there had him riding in circles. Not that I blame him. I saw her once."

He smiled slightly in memory, a hungry move of thin lips. Then he caught himself.

"I guess Orin wasn't the only one who chased her. He was knifed one night down there, just before Blaine came."

"I . . . see."

"It was a hell of a bad break for us," Harris continued swiftly. "I'm still trying to find someone to take his place."

The manager pushed through the swing gate, held it for Brad. He led the way outside and to the small adobe house, unlocked the door. There was little to see beyond a few boxlike rooms, still filled with the possessions of the dead man. After a quick tour of the rooms, Brad returned to the front door with Harris. He looked about, then out the open door onto the barren plateau. He could easily understand how Cochran could have tolled off the guards, caught the superintendent. With no one else around, the rest had been easy, particularly with the keys — Brad frowned.

"Did Orin carry the strongroom keys on him?"

"Why . . . I doubt it. Neither do I carry them unless I leave the mine. Orin would do the same thing. We'd not leave them behind for anyone to find."

"Where did he keep them?"

"I have them now. But Orin hid them in there." Harris pointed to a bedroom.

Brad puffed out his cheeks as he expelled his breath. He finally nodded and thumbed his hat back from his forehead. "I guess I'll learn nothing more here — for now."

"I wish I could tell you more," Harris sighed. He locked the door after they stepped outside, looked around the area and sighed again. "The money's gone with Cochran, and there's not a chance in hell of catching either. You'll find out."

"We'll see," Brad answered shortly.

"Yes, you will." A slight hesitation and then. "Will you be up here again?"

"Probably."

"And that's more trouble for me. My boys will head across the border at first sight of that badge and stay there until you're gone."

"Looks like you're closed down now."

"A holiday for some saint or other across the border. We'll be going full blast tomorrow." Harris gnawed at his lip a moment. "Look, Ranger, everyone's done all that can be done. I want to get back in full production. Our loss is covered by insurance, I checked that with a wire to our home office in San Francisco. So, it'd be best just to let the whole thing go."

"Your company agrees to that!"

"They do — at least that we not be pestered up here by lawmen. Man, there's ore that has to be brought out! We're thinking of that."

"So you'd let an outlaw just ride off?"

Harris made an irritable gesture. "Understand me — and the Company. We're for law and order. We'd like to recover the loss, sure. But we know we'll do that through insurance. But we don't want to lose a lot more by being shut down. Does that make it clear?"

"In a way," Brad conceded.

"You've had a long ride for nothing. I think, under the circumstances, the Company should make good the Territory's expenses. That would only be fair."

"You want me to ride off?"

Harris smiled tightly. "You make it hard, Ranger. Maybe we'd best forget it for a time. I don't want you to have wrong ideas about me or the Company."

Brad made a slight move of the head in agreement. "I'll try not to."

"Good." Harris walked with him to the horse tied to the rack before the office. As Brad started to mount, Harris checked him. "If you look around — oh, for a day or two — and decide I'm right, let me know. We could figure up how much the Rangers have spent on you and I'd send it — or give it to you, with a bit more for your personal trouble."

Brad half turned, angered, and then an inner caution made him swiftly hide it. He swiped his hand across his sweating lips and lifted his shoulders, let them drop. "You'll be around — if I need you?"

"Of course! Just send word and I'll meet you in town anytime. Or here, if you prefer. I reckon one visit won't upset my Mexes too much."

Brad swung into saddle and looked down at Harris' expectant face. He briefly touched his hatbrim, neck-reined the horse, and ambled back across the plateau toward the canyon that would lead to Piedra Mala. He didn't look back, but he knew that Harris had not moved.

At last he rode into the canyon and out of sight of the mine. He slouched in the saddle, then, and let the horse have the reins. His eyes grew distant and thoughtful, hardly seeing the slow passage of the rock walls on either side.

He reviewed what Harris had told him of the robbery. It had been so simple and easy — too easy! and Brad wondered that Blaine had not suggested as much. Cochran knew exactly when to hit the mine, when but three men were there. Of course, he could have watched the routine for a long time to know this. Brad shook his head. He had a hunch to rule that out.

For one thing, Cochran knew where the strongroom keys would be. No mention of forcing it out of Orin, the superintendent. Harris had said the man had been knocked out, and the outlaws moved with a precise knowledge. Harris had not said that they had, but Brad could see it. Then, this business of taking the loss — covered by insurance — reimbursing the Rangers.

Brad grunted angrily. Send it back with him with a little personal to boot. A bribe, covered with a specious sort of argument that gave Brad the hint. Just ride out, report failure, and he'd have money in his pocket. Or loaf around Piedra Mala for a reasonable time, pocket Harris' money, and ride out.

What kind of a man did Harris take him to be! A damned fool! This whole business had a carrion stink about it, and Brad wondered how much Harris was implicated. Yet, Brad cautioned himself, it made no sense for Harris to rob his own mine. But suppose he had — for whatever reason?

Brad's eyes narrowed. This would explain a lot, the veiled offer to him and, before that, Blaine's failure to find even a trace of Juan Cochran. Of course, Piedra Mala was the outlaw's haven, the way it worked out.

Suddenly Brad's anger dropped away, vanished as a new train of thought spun through his mind. Actually, it would be so easy to do as Harris suggested, and Brad would be the richer for it. Even more, if Harris was implicated, then Brad could up the ante for silence as well as for riding off. He'd have to get the proof, of course, and —

"Good God!" Brad exclaimed aloud in disgust at himself. Here he considered the very thing he had always completely rejected. What point to reject Waco Mead's offer and consider this one? At least the bounty hunter worked somewhere near the law.

There'd been too much pressure of late. First Joanie, then Waco, and — he heard Mary Alma's voice again — a lovely woman who'd had too hard a time to consider a Ranger with no more than his salary in his pockets.

Brad felt a shock at the thought. What made him think of the woman in that vein? He shook his head, clearing it. The heat, he thought wryly, and then wondered if Joanie's loss had bothered him more than he believed, making him instinctively look more awarely at the first beautiful woman he met. He pushed the bothersome thought from his mind and turned again to Harris.

If anything, the return journey was hotter than before. Long afternoon slant of the sunrays blasted at him like flames from an open furnace door. He hunched his shoulders against it, hat pulled low, swayed in the saddle, too enervated to think coherently about Cochran and the Golden Eagle Mine.

When he emerged from the last canyon and started down the slope toward the town, there was some relief. Rock walls had trapped the heat, but out here there was a faint stir of air. He straightened a bit, peered ahead down the last stretch of road, glad to see the end of his journey.

Later, when he emerged from the livery stable, he started toward the hotel. He recalled the room, and abruptly changed his direction, heading toward the saloon. He passed the café and gave a sharp, searching glance at the window. It reflected sunglare, and he could not see within. Slightly disappointed, he walked on and pushed through the saloon batwings.

It took a moment for his eyes to adjust to the dark interior. Then the bar and the tables came in focus. He pulled off his hat, mopped sweat from his forehead, grateful for the comparative coolness. He crossed to the bar, ordered a drink, took bottle and glass to the nearest table, and dropped into a chair.

He and the bartender were alone. Brad stretched out long legs, feeling the sweat around his belt and beneath his shirt. He sipped his drink, feeling weariness begin to flow out of his muscles. The bartender looked curiously at him, hesitated, and then broke the silence. "Looks like you had a mean ride, Ranger."

Brad nodded. "I've never seen country as hot as this."

"Ain't that a fact! Wasn't for the mine and ranches about no one would be loco enough to live here. If I could sell this place, I'd be gone like a shot myself."

Brad made no comment, and the bartender, garrulous through boredom, continued, "And I ain't the only one thinks that way. You take Mary Alma —"

Brad's head lifted slightly as the man continued without noticing, "— anyone make's a halfway decent offer for that place of hers, she'd grab it. But there ain't many fools around and none that drift in."

"Well, you both make a living," Brad hazarded.

"Yeah, of a sorts . . . me more'n her. Feel sorry for Mary. She belongs up Tucson way, or in some big town."

"What brought her here?"

"Husband came down with some idea of prospecting up in the hills, maybe a little ranching if he could get a start. I reckon Mary soon seen how slim both those chances were. Greg — that was her husband — was stubborn and wouldn't move on. She took what money they had and bought old Perez' hash house over there. Greatest thing happened to the town, Ranger! Her cooking after that other mess of grease Perez called food. She made a go of it. Then Greg got killed up at the mine. So, she's stuck. But I bet you if some gent rode in — one she could tell was decent, of course — and offered to take her away, she'd marry him and ride off."

Brad's eyes lighted a moment, and then he grinned crookedly to himself. Just then the batwings swung open, and Brad's thoughts broke off as he looked around. Hank Lewis stepped into the room, stood a moment, and then moved forward. He saw Brad and he gave a cool nod as he went on to the bar. He ordered, half-turned, leaning on the counter as he sipped his drink.

He caught Brad's glance and grinned. "Well, Ranger, have a good trip?"

"Good enough."

Lewis looked faintly and sardonically

surprised. He pushed from the bar and dropped down at the table without invitation. "Did you catch Cochran?"

Brad refused the bait for anger, answered evenly, "I never saw him."

"The way you rode in all frazzled, I thought you'd chased him all over the hills."

Brad's eyes flashed, but he said nothing. Lewis dropped back in the chair, light glinting from his badge, startling against the black shirt. "But I guess, being a Ranger, you learned a lot more about that robbery than a sheriff or a marshal would."

"I talked to Harris, looked around."

"My! You Rangers! Think of that!"

Brad finished his drink. "Marshal, I'm going to let you in on part of my plans."

"Well, now!"

"That's right — the way I'm going to wind up this business down here." Brad stood up and leaned across the table over the man, eyes locking with his. "Last thing I'm going to do, is pull you out from behind that badge and see if the rest of you fits your mouth."

He straightened, smiled easily. "Thought you might like to know."

Lewis sat with mouth open, eyes ablaze as he searched for words. Brad turned and strode away, leaving the marshal fuming. As

Brad pushed through the batwings, he felt as though some of the day's frustrations had been lifted from his shoulders.

At dusk, Brad bathed as best he could in the tepid water from the huge ornate pitcher and basin in his room. He escaped the box-like heat trap of the room as quickly as he could, and went out into the street.

The western sky showed red and gold, and purple shadows roiled and crept through the town, smoothing out the ugliness of the buildings, making the gaunt mountains look less repellent. Lamplight glowed here and there, but Brad moved toward one in the café. He saw horses now at the saloon hitchrack and faintly wondered that this parched land could sustain ranches and their riders.

Mary Alma, at first glance, appeared more lovely under the yellow glow from the lamps. But as she came up to the table and the light fell just right, Brad saw the lines of weariness about her lips and in the corners of her eyes. But she gave him a welcoming smile, forcing it through the fatigue.

"I'm late, I reckon," Brad said.

"That's all right. There's enough left for you."

He ordered, and she soon brought the food. She disappeared into the kitchen, and he heard her working back there as he ate. She returned as he finished, asked if he wanted pie. He started to agree, then asked sharply, "When do you close?"

"About now, maybe a little earlier. It doesn't matter."

"I think it does. You're tired."

"Oh, that's nothing new."

He shook his head and paid her. She accepted, too weary to press him. He picked up his hat, said goodnight, and she answered with a smile. She walked with him to the door, locked it after him when he went out. He stood looking back in the window, saw her gather up his dishes and walk slowly to the kitchen and disappear. Brad shook his head, sympathizing, and then strolled across the street to the hotel.

There were several riders now in the dark street, and Brad heard a burst of laughter from the saloon. He passed several Mexicans, men who caught the glint of his badge and moved swiftly away, eyes gleaming in the darkness.

He climbed the steps to the hotel porch, saw the fat man lolled in a chair by the rail. Brad dropped into the one next to him, and the man said, "Feels like it's twenty degrees cooler out here. Man's a fool to go inside until near dawn."

Brad watched shadowy riders pass in the street, men on the sidewalks. These were hardly more than moving shadows under the wooden canopies of the stores. He said,

"I didn't know there was this much life in the town."

"Dark brings 'em out. Oh, by the way, another stranger rode in a while ago. Registered, and then went to the saloon."

Brad kept his voice casual. "Who?"

"Name of Mead," the fat man answered. Brad said nothing, and a moment later, the man added, "Feller asked for you — a Mexican."

"For me?"

"Said he was from the mine. I told him you'd gone to Mary Alma's."

"He wasn't there."

"At the saloon then."

Brad wondered why a stranger in this town should ask for him, unless Harris had sent some message. Yet that seemed unlikely, considering what had transpired today. Brad dismissed the incident for the moment and looked toward the saloon, thinking of Waco Mead. The bounty hunter would be waiting for Brad's decision.

He stood up, thinking there would be no point in deferring his answer. Mead's proposal was just another in this recent string of incidents that tried to undermine Brad's way of living and working, his sense of the fitness of things.

He moved down the hotel steps to the street and worked his way across to the saloon, walking slowly. Mead would probably bring up arguments, Brad knew. Maybe the man would be right, for right now Brad wasn't so sure himself.

He came into the swath of lamplight that streamed out around the batwings. A man coming out was darkly silhouetted against the light, no more than a black outline, though Brad himself stood fully bathed in the lamplight's yellow glow.

The figure abruptly checked and Waco's voice boomed. "Just going to track you down. How about —"

The roar of the gun drowned him out. Brad felt the whistle and whip of the bullet by his face, heard its dull, deadly smack into the adobe of the saloon wall.

# Chapter Seven

Brad whirled around and dropped into a crouch as his hand whipped to his holster and the Colt blurred out. Waco threw himself to one side out of the light that framed him. Both men moved instantly with the speed of men trained to meet danger. A second shot blasted, and Brad saw the lance of flame from the corner of the building. His and Waco's guns answered with a double thunder.

Brad dimly heard shouts of alarm along the dark street, a chair crash within the saloon. He threw another slug toward the unseen assailant, and lunged forward in a low crouch. He lost track of Mead as, every nerve and sense concentrated, he reached the corner of the building.

A wide, dark passageway led back between the saloon and the store building just beyond. He half expected to find the bush-whacker down with a bullet, but the entrance to the passageway was clear. He dimly heard Waco's call. "Did you get him?"

Then, at the far end of the passage, flame blossomed again. The bullet sped wide, the man down there getting off a hasty shot. Brad fired in answer, the thought speeding through his mind that the man down there had suddenly panicked. He could have slipped away in the darkness but —

Waco's voice cut through the thought. "I'll circle, Nolan. Keep him nailed down."

Brad had flattened himself against the wall, gun held poised, ready to drop and fire. He now moved swiftly down the passageway, a flitting shadow that would make no target at all. He sensed, rather than knew, that Waco had sped around the other side of the saloon, and Brad's lips set in the grim line of the manhunter.

He broke out into the dark area beyond the saloon. He came to a halt, listening. He heard muffled sounds from within the saloon, faint alarmed voices from the street beyond. Then, out ahead somewhere, he heard the faint sound of flight. At that moment, Waco's shadowy figure appeared on the far side of the building.

"He's ahead," Brad called. "Running."

Ranger and bounty hunter raced after the unknown gunman, Waco bearing off to the left as Brad lunged straight ahead. Brad saw the dark shapes of adobes and shacks, a steady spray of lamplight from a distant window.

Suddenly, Waco's gun blazed. Brad instantly whipped in that direction. He had taken no more than half a dozen steps when a shadow rushed toward him. At the same instant, the man saw him. Brad faded to one side as his gun dropped and leveled. As he pulled the trigger, flame lanced toward him. Under the thunder, he heard a choking scream, and the shadow so close ahead crumpled and disappeared.

Brad remained crouched, gun hammer dogged back ready to drop. He heard no sound and slowly straightened as Waco called. "Nolan?"

"Okay, we got him — dead or wounded."

Brad eased forward as he heard Waco's hurrying steps grow louder. Then he saw the sprawled shape on the ground just ahead. Brad, gun held ready, stepped forward. The figure did not move. Waco appeared out of the darkness, came up sharp when he also saw the figure.

"Keep your gun on him," Brad said. "I'm getting a match."

The two men stood over the man at their feet. Brad struck a light, and the flame held steady in the still, hot air. He saw a dark face, mouth agape, eyes staring sightlessly upward and reflecting the brief flame of the match. He saw a dark stain on the shirt front and then the flame burned out.

Waco holstered his gun, said quietly, "Whatever chips he had, he's lost 'em. Who is he?"

"I don't know."

"He sure had no love for you."

Behind them a voice called, "Out there! What's happened?"

Brad looked over his shoulder toward the distant saloon. "Who's that?"

"Hank Lewis."

Brad grunted and then called, "Bring a lantern, Marshal. There's a dead man here. The shooting's over."

Shadows instantly stirred and voices lifted. Numerous boots thudded closer, and Brad then saw the curious crowd shape up out of the darkness. Lewis spoke in a strained voice, "Who are you? What's this about?"

"Ranger Nolan. It was a bushwhack."

"Oh, you!" Lewis snapped and came up, peering toward Brad. Then he saw the shape on the ground. "Who's that?"

Brad struck a match and held it above the dark, slack face. Beyond the crowd a lantern bobbed as a man raced forward. The match flame went out. "Know him, marshal?"

"I've seen him," Lewis answered with a faint note of reluctance.

The crowd parted to admit the man with the lantern to the inner circle. Lewis took it and placed it on the ground close to the dead man. In the steady light, Brad saw a coarse, pockmarked face, a shirt stiff with dirt, grease, and now dried blood. The man's holster was empty, but someone just then held out a Colt that had fallen a few feet away.

Brad looked up and around at the curious faces of the townsmen. "Anyone know him?"

"Louis Cardonez," someone volunteered.

The fat hotel owner pushed forward. "That's the one who was asking for you, Nolan."

"Well," Brad said grimly, "he found me."

"His bad luck," someone commented.

Brad straightened, looked at Lewis. "Maybe we should have a talk after you've taken care of this."

Lewis said nothing for a second, and then gave an order over his shoulder. "Some of you take him to Joe."

He made a gesture to Brad, and turned on his heel, walked through the crowd. Brad followed, Waco Mead close behind. The marshal silently led the way through the night to the dark buildings, along a passage between two of them, and into the street. He walked with an angry set to his shoulders, head thrust slightly forward. He entered his office, the door standing open, and turned up the wick of the lamp that burned in a wall bracket.

He turned then and asked sharply, "Now what's there to talk about?"

"A dead man and a try at murder," Brad answered and dropped unbidden in a chair before the desk.

"I know nothing about it," Lewis snapped, and then his cold eyes rested on Mead, who leaned against the wall just inside the door. "Who are you?"

"Waco Mead."

"Drifter?"

Brad cut in. "I'll vouch for Mead. Without him, there could've been a different story tonight."

Lewis' lips pulled back. "This is my town, Ranger, even though you might not think so. I like to know who rides in. Maybe Mead satisfies you but —"

"Did Louis Cardonez?" Brad snapped.

The marshal sat down behind his desk, obviously holding himself in check. His voice shook slightly, "I get the idea you tie me in with this business, Nolan."

"No, I still believe what your badge says — until you make me change my mind." Lewis started to speak, but Brad checked him. "You've made it clear you don't want me around. I figure it's jealousy of a kind. I've hit it before. But whether you like me or not, Cardonez made a try for me and damn' near made it. You act like that's not important. I wonder why?"

Lewis growled, "I didn't say that."

"My mistake then. So, let's start over. You know Cardonez?"

"He rides in and out now and then."

"Who was he?"

Lewis shrugged. "I never asked."

"A friend of Juan Cochran's? One of his bunch?"

Lewis hesitated. "I've seen him with Cochran's men now and then. I don't know that he's one of them."

Waco shifted his weight and Brad considered Lewis, then abruptly shot the question, "Why did Cardonez come gunning for me?"

Lewis flared, "How would I know! You figure I'm outlaw or something?"

Brad ignored the question, leaned forward. "The whole town knows why I'm here. Now, take what's happened. You'll not give me one bit of help — and you wear a badge. Harris, up at the mine, all of a sudden wants to forget the whole thing. Cardonez tries for me. You buck at answering questions straight."

"I've told you what I know."

Brad dropped back in his chair, sighed, seeing the uselessness of pursuing this course. "All right, marshal, now tell me what you plan to do?"

"What do you mean?"

"You as much as told me, and I heard around town, that you and Juan Cochran have a working agreement. So long as he and his bunch keep the peace in Piedra Mala, you figure he's no problem of yours. I'd say he broke that agreement tonight. So — where do you stand?"

Lewis flushed slightly, and then his jaw set. "Louis Cardonez ain't Juan Cochran. There's no proof Juan's behind this."

Brad shot a glance at Mead, and then slowly stood up.

"I guess that's clear enough." He walked to the door, turned. "Next time you see Juan Cochran, tell him Piedra Mala's unhealthy for him or any of his bunch. I'll arrest any of them or gun them down if I learn any of them ride in."

Lewis shot to his feet. "Like hell you will!

This is my town and —"

"This is Arizona Territory, marshal," Brad thundered. He touched his badge. "I've the authority to keep the Territorial peace anywhere. If you interfere, you'll wish you hadn't. Do we understand one another!"

Lewis stood with suffused face and clenched fists. Brad said tightly, "Pass the word."

He strode out, Waco swinging around and following after him.

Not long after, Brad lit the lamp in his room and Waco dropped on the bed, mopping the sweat from his forehead. He glanced toward the open window, in which came the sounds of the street just below. Brad caught the meaning of the look and said, "We're safe enough tonight."

"*You* might be," Waco corrected. "You're the one with the Ranger badge. They don't know about me yet. And I'd not be so sure about tonight if I were you."

"I figure Cardonez played a lone hand. Cochran won't know about him yet."

Waco grunted. "Just don't frame yourself in the window. I'd give odds Cochran knows by now. I figure he's just over the border."

Brad stood a moment, bemused, and then blew out the lamp. He heard Waco's sigh of relief, then a dry chuckle. "It took you just one day to stir things up and get yourself all measured for a tombstone. Still want to play a lone hand?"

Brad pulled the single chair to the window and sat down, looking out into the darkened street. He sat a bit back within the room, a mere shadow and poor target. The excitement caused by the shooting had died down and, so far as Brad could see, the scant night life of the town had returned to normal. Now and then a man entered or left the saloon, the stores were all dark except for the cone of light before the livery stable, the faint glow from the marshal's office.

Waco broke the silence. "How do you plan to get Cochran?"

Brad sighed. "If he's over the border, I'll wire to Tucson to clear me with the Rurales so I can go after him."

"Time," Waco said, "and you stack the chips against yourself. The next ambusher won't make mistakes."

"It's the only way," Brad said shortly.

"My offer still goes, Brad. And you're a man in need of lots of help. Lewis would be happy to stand around and watch you die. You threw a challenge at Cochran tonight that he don't dare pass up. If you bluff him, Cochran knows one of his men would figure he's running scared. How long would Cochran last before he'd have one of his own to face over a gun? Nope, Cochran's hide depends on his getting yours first."

"I could use help," Brad admitted.

"So do I, to wind this one up in a hurry. Throw in."

"I don't like bounty money."

"Oh, hell, that word's still sticking in your craw!" Waco exclaimed. "Say it is. We can still work together."

"How?"

"Helping one another when we can. I'll get the Mexican clearance from Tucson and —"

"No good, Brad. Red tape both sides of the border could take weeks or a month. I can't wait. I'd rather take the chances going alone over the border after Cochran. I'd feel better if you were along but, no. . . ."

"What else can I do?"

"Take that badge off your shirt and leave it here. We go after Cochran free of rules and red tape. In three days at the most, we'll be back with Cochran dead or alive. Either way, you've done your job, I've got my reward money. We both win, and we're both the richer — and who's to know in Tucson how you did the job?"

"No one, I guess," Brad said slowly. "Still —"

Waco arose from the bed. "Tomorrow, come dusk, I ride over the border. I'll have a partner, or I won't. You can come along, or you can stay here and watch for a bullet anytime or anyplace. Your decision. Ride with me, or forget the whole deal. Right now, I'm going to try to get some sleep in this flea trap of a hotel. Good night."

He moved out of the room, and Brad heard his steps fade down the hall.

# Chapter Eight

Despite the heat, Brad deliberately remained late in his room the next morning. He heard the town stir and come alive and, even at that hour of the morning, the sun blazed warm and threatening outside his window. He knew that Waco Mead would follow the pattern of early rising, and Brad did not yet want to give his decision.

He remained stretched out on the bed, listening to an occasional tread of boots by his door, hearing morning greetings outside as men prepared to record another day in the dreary history of Piedra Mala.

He stared up at the ceiling, and his mind lazily but carefully went over the items he had learned yesterday. How could he check on Dean Harris, the manager? And what about the knifing of the superintendent? It could easily be over a woman down there, Brad acknowledged to himself, but the timing seemed just too pat. Whatever the man knew about the robbery died with him. And that attempt to gun Brad down last night? Had Cardonez moved on his own, or had Juan Cochran himself planned it? Brad inclined to the last guess, but that meant Cochran had trailed Brad the whole day, from the moment he had arrived in town, to the mine and —

Brad blinked at the new thought. Had Harris' bribe and his failure to accept it made the outlaw move to have him killed? Brad grimaced, sat up, and swung his long legs over the side of the bed. He kept coming back to Dean Harris. And — where did Marshal Lewis fit in this situation? It was one thing to keep the peace in a town, but quite another to keep it by some sort of a deal with an outlaw. And where had Lewis been during the shooting? At the first gun explosion, most lawmen would have been right on the scene.

Brad arose and stretched, glanced out on the street below. Stores had opened, and a few people moved here and there under the wooden canopies. A rider, shoulders bent to sun, ambled northward by the hotel. Brad started to turn away but checked. Waco Mead appeared below him.

The bounty hunter strolled across the street and disappeared into the livery stable.

Brad waited, stepping back from the window. In a few moments, Waco led his saddled horse out, mounted and rode southward, toward the border. When he had disappeared, Brad turned to the washbowl, eager now to prepare for his own day.

A short time later, he emerged from the hotel, and went immediately to the café. By this time, the merchants had long since breakfasted, and Brad found the pleasant room to himself. Mary Alma appeared the moment the little bell over the door tinkled when Brad entered. She stopped short when she saw him, framed in the kitchen doorway. She wore a light blue dress this morning that seemed to compliment the color of her eyes that now looked at him with a personal warmth that surprised Brad. She caught herself, hastily smoothed her apron, and came forward as Brad sat down at one of the tables.

"Good morning," she said, "and I'm glad to be able to say it."

"Ma'am?"

"I heard about the gunfight last night. It's all over town. I wondered if you'd been hurt."

He smiled, "Thank you for the worry, but I was lucky."

"Indeed you were!" She avoided his eyes,

flushed slightly, and gave the breakfast menu. Brad ordered, and she disappeared. He looked after her, feeling a new warmth and pleasure at her interest. She soon returned with his eggs, ham, and biscuits, placed them before him. "I'll draw your coffee."

He obeyed a bold impulse. "And how about one for yourself?"

She hesitated, then smiled. "I guess I could."

She returned with the filled mugs, took a chair across from him with a sigh that Brad caught. "You work alone here — all day?"

"I have an Indian woman for the dishes and rough work. I do the rest."

Brad tackled his breakfast as he talked. "Sounds like crack of dawn to drop of night."

She nodded, added, "I come early to get the day's cooking started before the breakfast rush — if there is any. Noon dinners and night suppers keep me moving between stove and serving. Oh, I'm glad enough to see the day end."

She sipped her coffee, and Brad could see she enjoyed the respite. He heard faint sounds from the kitchen, assumed it was the Indian woman. A moment later, Mary confirmed it, "If Juana wasn't peeling potatoes back there, I'd not have this breather."

Brad made a slight gesture with his fork. "Does it pay enough for all that work?"

"I make a living of a sorts. Anyhow, I don't see much chance of getting away from it." She smiled. "Would you like to buy a restaurant?"

"Ma'am, I wouldn't know what to do with it. But how come you did?"

She drank slowly, and Brad felt she wouldn't answer him. Then she lowered her cup, and her lips made a lovely, expressive move. "I had the hunch to buy it while Greg was still alive. He was my husband. We didn't have much, but Old Perez was tired and sold cheaply. I guess I figured it as sort of insurance."

His lifted brow asked his question and she answered. "My husband was a good man and I loved him. But he was one with all sorts of notions and ideas. None of them made a lot of money, and most of them failed. We had money from some horse dealing Greg had made over in New Mexico. Then he came here with the idea of prospecting — or buying a small ranch."

She stared distantly out the window, eyes on the street, but thoughts in the past. "A man in this country has to have a lot of money to start a ranch and keep alive while he's building it up and fighting off rustlers with a full crew. Greg didn't have that much. Prospecting — he knew there was gold somewhere around besides in the Golden Eagle Mine, but Greg had no real idea how to find it. But he tried, give him credit."

She stopped, Brad waited, and, in a moment, she continued. "But that's all — no gold. He finally went to work at the Golden Eagle, and that killed him."

Brad, thinking of Harris and Cochran, asked sharply, "How?"

"Cave-in while they were timbering up." She looked around, suddenly in the present again, "Thank heavens, I had this!"

Brad pushed his plate aside and drank his coffee. "Lucky you had the hunch."

"Indeed!" She made a little face. "But here I am in Piedra Mala and here I'll stay."

"Oh," Brad said with an easiness he didn't feel, "maybe someone will come along. You'll marry again."

"Perhaps. But, much as I loved Greg, I won't marry another like him. Perhaps that sounds hard, but I've learned a lesson. Dreams and love are fine, but I believe they can be had with money as well as without. Oh, not a lot of money, but a good and steady job — a safe one. Or maybe a small spread in a country where a ranch can hold its own."

"An idea," Brad said.

She stood up. "Perhaps — and maybe I'm wrong. But until that's proven, I'll stick with the idea. More coffee?"

"No — thanks." She started to move off, but he checked her. "Your husband worked up at the mine. Did he know Harris?"

"Of course! Everyone does. He comes to town on weekends. You'll see him around. Now and then he makes a trip up to Cochise Springs — just to get away from this country, I suppose."

"Heard the superintendent was killed."

Her eyes darkened. "Yes, down in Mexico. He was a steady, dependable man — always nice to Greg. He came in here. I never heard he crossed the border until I learned he'd been killed down there."

"A knifing — over a woman," Brad said.

"That surprises me. I didn't think he'd be that kind of a man."

Brad rubbed his hand along his cheek. "Do you know if he and Harris got along?" Her eyes widened in surprise at the question, and then she frowned slightly. "So far as I know . . . but the last time he was here — No, I imagined it."

"What?"

"Nothing, really, except he said Hank Lewis was a fool and someday he'd learn to listen to people. I'd never seen Orin mad before."

"Right after the mine robbery?" Brad asked sharply.

"Yes, come to think of it."

Brad nodded his thanks and caught her curious look. He smiled slightly. "I suppose a lawman's always curious — about little things as well as big."

"You'd have to be." Her eyes dropped to his badge, lifted. "You've been called in about the robbery because Blaine couldn't handle it and Lewis won't."

"Well, yes. Marshal Lewis would have no right, though. It's the sheriff's job — or mine, now."

"I never thought of that, just that Juan Cochran and Hank seem to get along so well."

"I've heard."

He nodded and started to turn, but now she checked him. "I hope you don't mind — but do be careful. Last night — I heard the shots back in the kitchen. I heard you were mixed up in a gun fight. I was worried."

His face lighted and she flushed, spoke

sharply. "Like I'd worry about anyone I knew! But you must be after that outlaw, and last night was a part of it. Cochran is a deadly and treacherous man, Mr. Nolan."

"I can swear to that! You figure I'd be a poor bet for a gambling man?"

"One of the poorest, right now. I wouldn't want to be your wife for anything."

"I don't have one."

"Oh . . . well, then if you had one. . . ." She smiled in confusion, and covered it by sweeping the dishes off the table and retreating to the kitchen.

Brad went out onto the street, moving thoughtfully. He mentally repeated her words with his own variation. "A poor bet — for any woman." He grunted and jerked his hat low over stormy eyes. Give odds, something like that had influenced Joanie. No woman would want a man who could catch a bullet any day in the ordinary course of his job.

He pushed Joanie — and Mary Alma — out of his mind with an effort, looked toward the marshal's office, and then saw the fat hotel proprietor on his porch. Brad changed his course, knowing Lewis would not willingly talk about anything, including the weather.

A few moments later, he sat beside the fat

man, looking out on the nearly empty street. After a moment, he asked casually, "Does Dean Harris ever stop here?"

The moonface turned to him, showing surprise. "Not here! the saloon, yes. Goes to Cochise Springs about once a month, below the border as often as he comes to Piedra Mala. But stay in this hotel?"

He answered his question with a loud snort. Brad settled more deeply in his chair. "You don't like him."

"Didn't say that. He gets talking big when he drinks, but that ain't often. Always talks about the high-wide-and-handsome goings on he gets into in Cochise Springs. Some easy girls up there, I hear."

"But what's below the border?"

"Twenty miles of sand and cactus 'til you come to Callita. More women down there, I hear, and cantinas — and dollars buy a heap more'n they do up here."

"Did you know a man named Orin?"

"Sure, he come here now and then. Steady feller, Orin. Honest as they make 'em. Didn't like Harris and Harris didn't like him."

"Oh? How come he stayed on at the mine?"

"Heard Orin say once he was sent here by the Company. Reckon there wasn't much

Harris could do about it."

"When did he come?"

The fat man scratched one of his fleshy chins and squinted his eyes. "Four months ago, say. Give or take a week either way."

"I hear he went to Callita, too."

"Just once — and the last time. Killed down there."

"Over a woman."

"So I hear," the fat man replied in a tone that caused Brad to look around. The man grunted and pulled himself up in the slow manner of the overweight. "I guess it's right, though. Rurales brought the news."

He lumbered across the porch and into the lobby, leaving Brad seated on the porch. Brad slouched deeper in his chair, digesting the things he had learned. Now he'd bet he had a murder as well as a robbery on his hands, and one was tied in with the other. Only way to figure if what Mary Alma and the fat man knew about Orin was true — that and the timing of the killing.

He looked southward down the street toward Mexico. Everything seemed to point in that direction. And Waco Mead would ride there tonight, had gone out that direction this morning. Brad considered his next move. To go legally as a Ranger, he would have to ride first to the nearest telegraph at

Cochise Springs — a long trip north. He'd wire Tucson who, in turn, would go through the red tape of clearing with the Mexican authorities — and that could easily turn into a series of telegrams back and forth to Mexico City. In the meantime Brad would sit, waiting.

He stirred restlessly and his eyes came into focus. At that moment, Mary Alma hurried out of her little café and a few steps along the walk to the general store next door and disappeared. Brad sat quite still. She appeared briefly again, hurrying back to her café.

Brad said softly, "A poor bet. I'll always be."

He stood up and moved restlessly to the steps and down. He crossed the street to the saloon and entered. A few moments later, he leaned on the bar and stared deep into the untouched amber liquid in the shot glass. Once his hand half lifted to his badge, dropped away with a jerk. He came to a decision and downed the liquor in a single gulp, dropped coins on the bar.

He recrossed to the hotel, and settled once again in the chair under the wooden canopy. He half twisted about so that he faced south, waiting.

. . . For Waco Mead to return.

# Chapter Nine

As he had agreed with Waco, Brad waited until the bounty hunter had left the town and the first shadows of night crept around the buildings. He spent the time in the small café, giving himself the excuse that he could do with a final piece of pie and cup of coffee. It might be a long time before he could find something like that in Mexico.

To his chagrin, several townsmen had decided on late suppers, and he did not have the girl to himself. But she had given him a surprised and pleased smile when he came in so soon after his own meal. He watched her move about serving the others, and he suddenly wondered if he had made the right decision. Come down to it, he thought as he finished the last of the coffee, how could it matter to her what he did? He was just another customer who, she knew, would leave Piedra Mala when his job was done. The last taste of the coffee seemed bitter, and he hastily arose, paid, and left.

He saddled his horse, shoved rifle in the boot, and led the horse out the wide rear door. Not that Marshal Lewis would not hear about his leaving, but Brad did not want to be too conspicuous. He mounted, swung the horse north, and rode off. Far enough out that he could not be seen by curious or spying eyes, he cut away from the town, made a wide circle, and finally struck the narrow road heading south to Mexico.

He turned the horse into it, and rode slowly along, eyes probing into the starlit darkness. In less than five minutes, the shadowy shape of a rider appeared, and Waco hailed in a low, cautious voice. Brad answered, and the bounty hunter reined in beside him. Brad drew up.

Waco said, "Border's about fifty feet ahead, as I figure it. No marker you can see at night."

"How far's Callita?"

"I hear twenty miles." Waco hesitated. "You're still wearing the badge, friend."

Brad grunted. "Forget it."

He lifted his hand, and Waco said hastily, "You're sure you want the deal?"

"Certain."

"Okay." Waco neck-reined his horse. "You

got fifty feet if you want to change your mind."

He moved ahead as though to give Brad this last moment of privacy and decision. Brad followed after a moment's hesitation. He worked at the badge, and it seemed his fingers suddenly became awkward and fumbling. At last the badge loosened, and Brad slowly pulled it from his shirt. He had the strange sensation that his left breast became suddenly bare. He weighed the form of silver and nickel for a moment, and then abruptly thrust it into his trouser pocket. He felt the weight there more than he ever had on his shirt.

Waco reined in and let Brad come up. He peered sharply in the darkness, and then seemed to ease down in his saddle. His voice sounded casual. "I reckon we're on our own from here on. Did anyone see you leave Piedra Mala?"

"Probably — but I rode north."

Waco's teeth flashed faintly in the darkness. "Depend on a Ranger to know all the tricks."

"You forget — right now I'm not a Ranger."

"So I did. Well, let's ride south, pardner."

Brad touched spurs, and the two men rode on abreast. An illusion, of course, but

Brad felt he knew the exact instant they crossed an invisible line into illegality. At the same moment, he felt as though he himself had changed, inwardly. It had to do with a share of Waco's bounty money. It was crazy, but it was there and Brad could not quite shake it off.

Waco broke the silence of the night. "I rode about five miles or more down this way this morning. Sometimes the Rurales set up traps. Just about the time a border-jumper feels he's safe, they nail him."

Brad grunted. "Now that would be a real nice turn!"

"Bothersome, that's all. You left your law behind you — back there."

They rode on for a time, and then Waco said, "You know, I wouldn't have taken a bet either way about you."

"Why not? You argued hard enough."

"Sure, I needed you. But I still half expected to play a lone hand. How does it feel without a badge?"

Brad felt a flash of anger, feeling Waco might be expressing some inward triumph. But, thinking of the man's tone, Brad rejected the thought. "Funny — like a weight's gone."

"Well, now! It can't be more'n a few ounces."

"A lot more! A hell of a lot more!"

They rode alone through the darkness, and nothing moved but themselves. The distorted shape of a cactus would loom up out of shadows, seemed to silently threaten as they rode by, and then fade into darkness again behind them. They heard a scurry that alerted them both, and then the desert silence fell again. They rode on, hands dropping away from holstered gun, knowing some desert creature had fled at their approach.

Waco suddenly spoke, hesitantly. "Brad, maybe I didn't really know how much being a Ranger meant to you. A man like me, he goes by what gain he can see right in front of him until something brings him up short. Like you — right now."

"Me? I just agreed to throw in with you."

"Did you now? Just that? Money talks to me, friend, but now and then my ears catch something else. Nothing pleases me better than you riding beside me, but I'm curious what finally made you decide."

Brad found his mind suddenly touching on a dozen reasons, and combinations of them, and rejecting them. Waco would not really understand. It had to do with the past, and a feeling, an impulse. These things Waco would reject. Brad tried to put it in bold, harsh terms.

"You made me see I'm a manhunter, no different than you. It's all blood money, no matter how you look at it. So, I asked myself why I shouldn't take rewards — at least on this one."

Waco chuckled. "Money talks — I've always believed it."

"Don't it! Talks a badge right off a lawman! Talks in a whole new way of life."

Waco turned his head, startled. "What?"

"Soon as I finish this job and we've split the money, I'm doing something else. Find a place where land's cheap, or I can homestead. Crooked things there, too, when you come to think of it. I can hire a couple of riders and take out a section of homestead in each of their names. That's done, ain't it?"

"I've heard. Friend, you're really changing brands!"

"Two thousand dollars for Juan Cochran, and that's what I have to work with. Cut corners to stretch it out, but it can be done. I want a safe, respectable life . . . one that no woman will be afraid of if I find one I want to marry."

Waco made a long and surprised whistle. "That one you lost?"

"Not her. But she taught me I don't bring

much in the woman market. So. . . ."

His voice drifted off. The road they followed, no more than a gray uncertainty ahead of them, lifted up a small rise, and dipped again. They had only the dark land and the stars, and both felt a deep sense of isolation. It led to long silences, such as now fell on them. They rode up and over another long desert swell. At its peak, they saw only infinite darkness on every side.

Brad asked, "I heard there's a town of sorts near, where Harris' workers go."

"Over west. A dozen adobes around a ramshackle chapel. No more."

"It will be close to the line, and handy for Cochran."

"That it is, and he uses it as a place for his gang to kick up their heels in the cantinas and with what women there are. But Juan has his own hideout."

Brad said dryly, "You were busy this morning."

"Wandering around, friend. I'm a *gringo* drifter who can't stay too long in once place in the States. Juan Cochran might like to meet up with someone like that. Or so I heard in the village. Nothing definite, just guesses."

"Like where we can find him?"

"Well, maybe a little more. After I bought

drinks around and acted owl-hoot, those *bandidos* sort of warmed up. Figured I'd be wild enough for their bunch. Heard one say so, and he'd ride out to a place he called Lago Seco. It's somewhere south of the town, I figure two to five miles. We'll cut over that way soon, when I'm sure we're well below the village."

Brad tipped his hat back from his forehead to let the night breeze touch it. "Like I said, you were busy."

"Man without a badge moves free, friend."

They fell silent. Some miles further on, Waco drew rein and Brad pulled up beside him. The bounty hunter looked westward into the darkness for long moments and once his eyes turned in the direction they had come. Apparently satisfied, he made a gesture, and led the way off the poor road they had followed.

Now they moved west and slightly south. Brad fixed the position of a star and soon realized Waco had also done something like that. They moved steadily with hardly a noticeable drift in direction. The miles and time passed. They suddenly came upon another road, hardly more than a trail that they would have missed had not traffic grooved it into the desert floor.

Waco drew rein. "The town's north of us

now, maybe a mile. Lago Seco should be down this way, and I know this is the only road leading to it."

"Lago Seco, another *aldea*?"

"No, not a village, from what I could figure. A *ranchera,* maybe. South of us, anyhow."

"Then we head south," Brad reined his horse into the poor road, and Waco gigged his own to catch up.

Now they rode more slowly. The place they sought might be on the road or far off it, a secondary trail leading to it. Waco and Brad moved slightly off the road on either side, eyes casting ahead for light or the dark shape of a house, closer and to either side for sign of branch trail or sign. Brad discounted their luck in finding a sign along the road, that was an American custom.

They rode slowly now, and no sign of habitation or road broke the dark expanse of desert. No light gleamed afar off, and there was no travel along the road except themselves. Brad finally drew rein, and Waco crossed the road to him.

"We've come maybe four-five miles," Brad said. "We could ride right past it, maybe have."

"What do you think?" Waco asked.

"I'd say pull well off the road and wait

until dawn. At least we can see better and farther."

Waco sat silent a long time, his head turning slowly, eyes probing the darkness. At last he sighed, and Brad urged his horse off the road, Waco following. Some hundred yards further, Brad drew rein and swung out of the saddle.

"This'll do. Far enough out not to be seen, close enough to hear anyone along the road."

They made a dark and dry camp, picketing their horses, spreading blanket rolls, and spelling one another keeping watch during the night. The darkness wrapped about them, and Brad began to feel that the night would last forever.

He sat, during one of his turns, back against his saddle, legs stretched out on the blanket. A few feet away, Waco snored gently. Brad eased his position, glanced at the dark sky without real hope of seeing dawn. Suddenly, he had the strange sensation that he lived in a different and alien world, one in which he did not belong. It would be better if he had the badge on his shirt, if this was Arizona. But this was strange, a far-off planet, and he had no business being here. He had to fight down the impulse to awaken Waco, call off the deal, and ride north, where he belonged.

But, in the same instant, the wry and bitter thoughts that had trailed him all the way from Tucson and had forced him to a decision in Piedra Mala rose up to battle the impulse. Even so, he sat for a long time with fingers tightly intertwined, face muscles tight. The inward struggle seemed as endless as the night.

Suddenly he felt a freshening stir of air along his cheek, and the inner turmoil vanished. His head lifted, knowing he had felt the first stir of dawn breeze. He stood up, stretched cramped muscles, glad the interior struggle had not come to a decision; but yet he felt a subtle and bothersome sense of defeat.

He shrugged that off as he moved silently, turning to the east. The sky seemed pitch black, and yet he knew it was false. Not long after, he saw the subtle paling that seemed almost a trick straining eyes played on the mind. But it grew more substantial, and then the first paling began.

He bent to Waco, shook him. Mead snorted, rolled over, and sat up, instantly awake. Brad said, "It's dawning."

Waco stretched his arms wide, yawned, and then stood up. They went out to their horses, saddled up. By then, the eastern sky glowed palely, and now gaunt shadows of cactus and brush became more distinct. Gradually, the day crept toward them and they began to see the shape of the land.

They mounted and Brad indicated the top of a small hillock just ahead. They rode to the crest, and now day stood distinct, the golden and red glow of the climbing sun bright to the east. Brad looked slowly around, and suddenly pointed north.

"There. We passed it in the dark."

They could see it now, hardly more than a narrow horse trail cutting off from the main road and leading eastward toward a line of low, sandy hills. It disappeared between them.

"Lago Seco?" Mead asked.

"Dry pool," Brad translated. "Sort of fits what we're looking at."

He loosened the rifle in the scabbard and the Colt in his holster as he lightly touched spurs to the horse and led the way directly toward the hills. As they approached, Brad narrowly watched the point where the trail appeared, but he also searched the whole line of hummocks. He made a brief gesture toward another narrow passage between them, and Waco nodded.

Riding as they were now in the open, Brad knew they would be instantly spotted by anyone coming out of the hills along the road. Unlikely at this early hour, but still he didn't want to risk it. With a feeling of relief, Brad led the way into the second narrow swale between the hills, and they were hidden from chance discovery.

The way they came, twisted and turned erratically, and Brad knew why no trail came through here. But at last the low slopes began to fall away and Brad rode more slowly, eyes keened ahead, hand never far from his holster.

A tension came to both men as they sensed they neared the end of their search. There was a chance a guard would watch this pass, though this country was Cochran's secure base. Finally, they reined in at the open mouth of the swale.

The slope below them was gentle, sweeping down toward a grove of palo verde trees. They saw an adobe house, whitewash peeling, planked door closed, narrow windows dark at this distance. Brad sought for sign of life, saw none.

Waco indicated a spot off to the right. "Dry tank over there. See it? Fits the name."

Brad nodded. "No one moving. No horses. But they could be in that adobe beyond the main building."

"It's daylight. We could be seen if we drift in."

Brad indicated, with a jerk of the head, a direction to the right, toward the dry tank. "That's the blind side of the house. We can't sit here."

"It might work."

"Let's find out."

Brad moved out and at an angle toward the dry tank, eyes never leaving the adobe, its door, or its thick narrow windows.

# Chapter Ten

They moved swiftly, and the distant adobe seemed to wheel until it presented its blank side to them. Now they could see a portion of the rear yard, a small corral. Brad made a sound in his throat and indicated the four horses to Waco. "Figure one of 'em's Cochran's?"

"A chance." Waco added. "Four against two of us. We could have better odds in a showdown. Sure as hell, we're not just going to walk in and ride off with Cochran."

Brad drew rein, spoke dryly, "Did you expect to?"

"It has been done. But there was luck."

Brad considered the silent building, looked sharply at Waco. "You said some of Cochran's men figured you for their bunch. Maybe they'd like to add two of us to the gang."

Waco looked startled, then grinned. "It's worth a chance, friend."

Brad gave a slight nod, touched the horse into motion, and now rode directly toward the house, boldly approaching its door. He pulled in some distance out, cupped his hands about his mouth, and called. Both men sat at apparent ease in their saddles, but Brad knew Waco was as alert for trouble as he.

A long moment passed and again Brad called. They saw no movement, but suddenly a voice called from one of the deep-slitted windows. "What you want?"

Brad spoke to Waco in a low voice without turning his head. "They know you. Ride ahead."

Mead lifted the reins, shoved his hat back from his face so it could be plainly seen. He drifted forward. "I'm looking for a friend I met at the *aldea* yesterday. He said —"

Another voice lifted. "Hey, *amigo!* I tell Juan about you!"

The door suddenly opened, and a dark-skinned man stepped out. He was bareheaded, and Brad, even at the distance, saw the scar along one cheek. He wore a heavy cartridge belt, gun in its holster. Behind him, another man appeared in the doorway, then a third.

The first one advanced a step, and then pulled up short, suspicious eyes cutting to

Brad. "Who is that one?"

"Friend of mine," Waco answered easily and grinned crookedly. "He's looking for trouble, like me. We've rode some dark trails together, me'n him."

A fourth man appeared as the two in the doorway wandered slowly out. Brad's hopes fell as he knew the fourth could not be Juan Cochran. One of them spoke to Waco's friend, "Juan will not like this. You told this *hombre* too much . . . where to find him."

Waco spoke up quickly. "Not him. I figured it out from what I heard. Where's Cochran?"

"He will be here," his friend answered. "You wait, eh?"

"Manuel," one of the others cautioned, "how do we know who they are? Gringo lawmen, maybe?"

Manuel laughed, a low and mocking sound. "This side of Piedra Mala? Not them." He spoke to Waco, "The corral is in back. We will have something to eat, now you have awakened us."

Waco nodded and reined his horse around. Brad followed and Manuel sauntered more slowly. They had just reached the corner when an exclamation from one of the others brought them all around. The man pointed toward the low hills where the path debauched from them.

Brad saw a single rider coming at an easy canter. Manuel shaded his eyes, then dropped his hand and turned to Waco. "It is Gregorio. He is next to Juan. He will decide about you, pronto."

The rider came on, and the outlaws moved out to meet him. Brad and Waco remained in the saddle. The newcomer came closer, and now Brad could see he was slender and supple, dark eyes flashing and alert. A cartridge studded belt circled his waist, and he was dressed like a Mexican dandy, though trousers and shirt showed fading and wear. Long cruel spurs glinted in the sun from his soft boots.

Manuel called. "Eh, Gregorio! Here is the one I told you about."

Gregorio's eyes followed the sweep of Manuel's arm toward Waco, and then the man looked at Brad. He abruptly reined in with a savage jerk of the reins. His eyes narrowed, and then thin lips under equally thin mustache pulled back against his teeth. "Ranger! The one who killed Louis! That one — get him!"

His hand slashed to his gun. Manuel and the others stood transfixed a moment. But Brad and Waco exploded into motion. Brad's Colt blurred up out of the holster, and he slammed a shot at Gregorio. It whipped the high crowned hat from the man's head. At the same moment, Gregorio's gun and Waco's exploded simultaneously. The slug whipped by Brad's shoulder as Waco's bullet caught Gregorio and dumped him from the saddle.

Manuel yelled, dropped to a crouch. The other three, near the door grabbed for their guns. Brad's spurs raked his horse, and he threw a wild shot toward the group near the door. He raced toward the hills, heard Waco's wild yell and thunder of his gun, and then the roll of hoofs.

Bullets whipped high and to either side of Ranger and bounty hunter. Manuel's curse sounded clear, his shouted orders. Brad threw a glance over his shoulder. Gregorio, clutching his arm just above the elbow, sat up and spat curses and words that Brad could not hear above the thunder of hoofs and guns. But Manuel and his three companions broke in a run toward the corral.

Now the low hills loomed close and Waco, using spurs, came up beside Brad. He yelled. "Give 'em five minutes and we'll have the hornets after us."

"And a nest ahead — in the village — between us and the border."

They whipped through the low swale

between the hills and saw the main road, if such it could be called, ahead of them. Brad swiftly sought for other hills that might conceal their flight, but there were none. No matter which direction they rode, they would be in plain sight of their pursuers. The wider trail ahead, the north-south wagon track offered their best chance to make speed rather than the softer, uneven stretch of the desert to either side. Brad set his horse to it, Waco following.

They came to the road, turned into it, and Brad headed north. Waco just behind him yelled a warning. "The rest of the gang! In the village! We'll run right into them."

"Have to risk it. Shake our friends behind us, first."

Just then Waco, looking back, saw four riders stream out of the hills behind them and start in grim pursuit. He called a warning, and Brad waved his hand in acknowledgment. They set themselves to the flight. Brad heard guns fire behind him, but the slugs flew wide and wild. He did not waste time returning them.

On the slightly wider road, Brad and Waco sped side by side. Now and then Waco threw a look back. The low bushes and sand blurred by on either side. Brad looked ahead for first sight of the village, and then back at their pursuers. He could see Manuel leading the pack, the other three bunched just behind him.

Waco brought him around straight with a jerk. "There's the town! Caught a glimpse of it!"

Brad's lips thinned. Outlaws behind and outlaws ahead, perhaps Cochran himself. This trap threatened to close on them in a matter of minutes. He suddenly reined in and wheeled his horse about.

Waco cursed in surprise, but Brad snaked his rifle from its scabbard, jacked a shell in the chamber with almost one continuous motion. The weapon jumped to his shoulder, lined on the pursuing bandits, still beyond revolver range. The rifle spat a lance of flame. Manuel's horse went down in a lunging spill, throwing its rider over its head, in a dust-raising sprawl, into the road.

The three behind swiftly sawed back on the bits, and their mounts reared high. Brad threw another shot, with no intent to score, and the three whipped about. Brad saw Manuel groggily lift himself from the ground.

He sheathed the rifle. "That'll hold 'em back."

Waco threw a look toward the village ahead. "And rouse the hornets back there."

Brad nodded grimly, reined his horse off the road. "Circle it wide, or head for the Callita trail."

"Then let's ride," Waco snapped.

They headed east and north at an angle, their attention back on the road where their pursuers had been stopped. They saw the three come up to Manuel, who now stood up and gestured toward them. Waco, suddenly made a warning sound and flung his arm toward the village.

"They're swarming."

Brad saw a dozen riders stream out toward Manuel and his companions. Brad threw a flat, hard smile at Waco. "How many of them have rewards on their heads?"

"More'n we can collect — and stay alive."

Waco straightened and raked his spurs. He and Brad raced on over the uneven ground. Now and then they topped swells and could see, behind them, Manuel fire his gun in the air and wave his sombrero in the air toward them. The group from the village suddenly swerved and came pounding toward them.

Brad leaned slightly over his horse's head and Waco also bent to the rhythm of his speeding mount. They dropped into the hollow of the swale, and the scene behind them blotted out. Brad, slightly in the lead, swerved up the swale, and Waco followed. Now, out of sight of their pursuers, the change of direction gave them a chance to evade capture or an outlaw slug. Their way led north, and Brad threw a glance over his shoulder. Soft dust lifted behind the pounding hoofs of their horses, and he wondered if it would settle before the outlaws dropped into the swale and detected it.

He straightened, knowing this would be entirely up to chance and the gentle breeze. They pounded along, the low walls blurring by on either side. Brad saw a break in them, veered to it and scrambled up. Now they were out on the level, and he risked another look back.

His face became tight. Half the outlaw bunch from the village had ridden straight on, and Brad could see them some distance back and to the south. The other half had disappeared, and Brad knew they followed the swale. Whoever led them, probably Juan Cochran himself, had the shrewd cunning of the fox and had guessed Brad's maneuver. And then topped it by splitting his own men to form two arms of a pincer.

Waco rode slightly behind Brad. He suddenly straightened, staring ahead in alarm. Brad's head jerked around. He saw a dozen riders racing toward them, still too far to be distinguished. *A third bunch of outlaws!* flashed through his mind. He whipped directly north now in a desperate bid to escape this unexpected trap. Instantly three riders of the bunch ahead, cut out at a tangent from the main group, on a course that would head Brad and Waco off. The others raced straight ahead, fanning out.

Waco had dropped back slightly. He looked back, ahead, and suddenly savagely reined his horse directly west. Brad had not seen the move, intent on the three who, bent low and quirts working, raced to head him off. Brad could not go back. He would only run right into outlaw slugs from the two groups back there. Then he saw Waco racing off. At the same moment, beyond the bounty hunter, half a dozen riders lifted out of the swale. Brad knew Waco had no chance, and he yelled a warning; but Waco did not hear, merely desperately swerved his horse in yet another direction.

Brad realized that, for the moment, it was every man for himself. He might outdistance the three riders who tried to cut him off. It would be his only chance. He raked spurs and bent low over the horse's neck. The three ahead used quirts mercilessly, and their horses, in the distance, seemed to fairly flatten out in a burst of speed.

Suddenly, behind Brad, a burst of shots sounded. He thought of Waco and threw a swift look in that direction. Waco raced on but, beyond him, the outlaws had suddenly veered off in a wide circle, racing for the swale and dropping into its protection. Surprised, Brad looked back the other way. The new group of riders now raced directly for the outlaws. Brad saw puffs of smoke from Colts, saw the little lances of flame. Further back, the other group of outlaws broke course, made a tight circle, and fled.

He straightened, lifting his body to get a clearer look at the three who sought to cut him off. They sped toward him like three deadly arrows. Brad's hand dropped to his Colt, and then he caught a glint of metal as one of the men momentarily twisted about. A badge! Brad felt a momentary surge of relief, and then realized his own false position. He no more dared be captured by these lawmen than by the bandits!

But in that same instant, he realized his own momentary and instinctive slackening of pace had lost the race for him. The three swerved in on him. At the same instant, he heard a shout behind him and, a quick look over his shoulder revealed two more racing up.

He saw the glint of Colts, and now the badges and the marks of the uniforms. Brad reined in, knowing he was trapped. He lifted his hands high, holding his heaving horse in check by the pressure of his knees. He had faint hope that, his badge concealed, he might talk his way out of this. At least he had stopped a slug from tearing into his body.

Now the riders ahead, and those behind, slackened their headlong pace. Guns jumped into dark hands and leveled on him. The Rurales moved in, narrow-eyed and grim-faced.

# Chapter Eleven

Brad could only wait tensely. Off in the distance, he saw the others of this heavy patrol disappear into the swale in pursuit of the outlaws. Miraculously, Waco rode west and north, a black dot now, and unpursued. Then Brad's attention returned to the slowly closing ring of men.

He could now distinctly see the badge of authority on each dark jacket. One wore a gold insignia and moved with an air of assured authority. He came up, gun leveled. Dark eyes swept over Brad, lifted to his face, hard and probing. He spoke an order, and Brad heard a man move up behind him. His Colt suddenly lifted from the holster as a second Rurale came up and, leaning far out, pulled the rifle from the scabbard. Then the officer eased back and holstered his Colt.

He spoke in heavily accented English. "We've caught one of you, if no more."

"I'm no *bandido.*"

White teeth flashed in a sardonic grin. "Not down here, eh? Maybe we make you one, *amigo,* once we find out about you. How many places you wanted in America, eh?"

"No place. Look, Lieutenant, I was being chased by that bunch, me and my friend."

"So? Yet you run from us, eh? Now why is that?"

Brad's lips opened, snapped shut. He shrugged. "We figured you were just some more outlaws."

The officer's thin cheeks sucked in. He suddenly stood up in the stirrups and looked toward the swales. A thin tracery of dust at some distance showed the invisible path of the pursuit. Afar off, hardly more than a speck now, Waco Mead headed fast toward the horizon.

The officer eased down into the saddle, faced Brad again. "Your name?" he snapped suddenly.

"Brad Nolan."

"From where?"

"Arizona Territory."

"What work do you do?"

"I'm —" Brad caught himself. "Rider, that's all."

"No more than that, eh?" The officer's dark eyes flicked to one of the Rurales.

"Search him — all pockets."
"Now look here! You can't do that!"
The tight smile flashed again. "No? What do you fear if you're just a rider, eh? Search him, Pedro!"
Brad stiffened and then knew the futility of protest or resistance. He submitted, arms still held high above his head. Hands patted trouser pockets, pulled out kerchief, knife, and leather purse. At a signal from the officer, the purse was opened, disclosing a few bills, some silver and gold coins.
"Return them. Search further," the young officer snapped.
Hands moved up to the twin flap pockets of Brad's shirt. The harsh, tight face of the Mexican Rurale was but inches from his own, the dark eyes heavy with silent warning not to move. But the Colts in the hands of the others in the ring about Brad was warning enough. The hands patted one pocket, empty — then the other. Brad felt the sharp pressure of the badge against his chest as the man's fingers touched it, pressed a second, and then swiftly dipped into the pocket.
He held the silver badge in a dark hand toward the Rurale officer. The young man studied it with a strange lack of surprise. His eyes slowly lifted and Brad caught the

deep gleam of satisfaction "Ranger, eh? Is this why the *bandidos* chase you?"

Brad moistened his lips, then nodded. "That's why. Look, we're both lawmen, and these arms are getting mighty sore up like this."

"Of course, courtesy of Rurale to Ranger, eh? You may drop them, *amigo.*" But no real friendliness showed in his face as he watched Brad lower his arms with a relieved sigh. "Now, perhaps, you can tell the truth, eh?"

Brad did not let the new tension, coming so soon after relief, show. "What do you mean?"

"That one," The officer's arm indicated Waco, far in the distance. "He is Ranger, too?"

"No, just me."

"This is Mexico, *amigo,* fifteen miles inside of it." The young man folded his hands over the high saddle horn and leaned forward slightly. "What is a Ranger doing here?"

Brad felt the increasing falseness of his position. If he hoped to complete this assignment with the arrest of Juan Cochran, he could not be jailed himself. He could imagine, with an inward shudder, the repercussions from here to Mexico City to

Tucson. Much as he disliked it, he had to be evasive with this young lawman of Mexico, whom he instinctively liked.

"I'm off duty. Just rode down here to see what the country's like. Met him —" his eyes cut beyond the officer. "And we tangled up with those outlaws."

Again, lean dark cheeks sucked in. "Arizona Ranger Nolan just take a ride, eh? And, by chance, he runs into Juan Cochran's band?"

He waited but Brad merely shrugged as though agreeing. The dark young face flamed with anger. "We had word, Ranger, that you had crossed the border. There has been nothing from Mexico City that you have permission." His voice softened silkily, "but, perhaps, you have such an authorization?"

Brad slowly shook his head. The officer straightened, made a sharp gesture to his men. "He is prisoner. We will take him with us."

"Lieutenant, now —"

*"Silencio!"*

One of the men produced handcuffs, and Brad stared at the officer. "Do you have to —"

The man reined about without a word and, a second later, a steel bracelet snapped about Brad's wrist. He sat manacled, hands on the saddle horn, holster and rifle scabbard empty, between two alert Rurales. At a sign from the officer, the small group rode to the swale and then along its brink in the direction the pursuit had taken. They rode slowly. Beyond it and at a distance, Brad saw the scattered adobe hovels and the shops around the plaza of the village.

They heard the sound of muffled hoofs in the swale, and the officer drew rein. They waited and, shortly, the rest of the Rurale patrol appeared, riding toward them, horses sweating. Even Brad could tell from their faces that the outlaws had escaped. He caught enough of the Spanish report to gather that the outlaws had suddenly scattered in every direction so that further chase had been fruitless.

The officer listened to the report in silence. He suddenly spat orders and the men fell in behind him as he rode down into the swale, up the other bank, and headed directly for the village. Brad's two guards rode close beside him in the fast canter, and the other lawmen rode behind him. Brad knew there was no chance of escape.

They came into the village. Only a mongrel dog greeted them with hysterically profane barking, and then tucked in its tail and fled. There was no other sign of life in the few adobes, nor in the baked earth plaza when the officer drew rein. He gestured toward a cantina.

Two of the men dismounted, hurried inside. They reappeared with a pockmarked, surly man between them, whom they shoved roughly to a rocking stand before the lieutenant. Questions and answers came so fast Brad couldn't fully follow them. The man shook his head stubbornly, shrugged, and scowled.

"Liar!" Brad caught that word from the officer, then a whole string of exploding, fiery syllables that made the villager cringe, scowl, and his eyes reflect suppressed fury. With a kicking, contemptuous motion of his spurred boot, the officer dismissed the man. The two Rurales spun him around, and one sent him sprawling toward the cantina with a well-placed kick. Grins flashed as the officer wheeled about and the rest followed him out of the village, Brad still captive in their midst.

They headed directly east, and Brad sensed he was being taken to Callita. The group rode steadily and silently, except for the creak of leather, an occasional snort from a horse. Just ahead of Brad, the officer rode slim, tall, and angrily, his shoulders well back, head high, the tall-crown sombrero almost like a banner.

The barren miles flowed by, and now Brad could see the type of country he and Waco had ridden last night. It was only a continuation of the repellent land around Piedra Mala except for the low, barren mountains just north of the border. Despite being a prisoner, Brad eyed these lawmen of Mexico professionally. He liked what he saw of them and approved, even though they were his captors. They had a pride, a spirit that he could sense. Not as good as the Rangers, he thought, with a touch of natural prejudice, but he gave them his respect.

After a long ride, the course changed slightly, and soon Brad saw the town ahead. It was of fair size, and he had seen the red-tiled spires of the church for many miles before he saw the lower adobes. These gradually lifted, it seemed, out of the desert floor, grew larger and at last the troop rode into the town. Here and there, curious people stopped to watch them pass, eyes widening as they saw the *Americano* prisoner among them.

They came into the plaza, the square lined with shops on three sides, the church on the fourth. The officer rode at an angle across the square to a low building with thick adobe walls.

Brad could see no bars, but something in its repellent shape, the narrow windows with thick embrasures, told him it was the town jail. The young officer dismounted, gestured Brad's guards to bring him in. The rest of the troop eased in the saddle, reaching for cigarettes. Brad dismounted and instantly one of the Rurales whirled him about and gave him a shove. Brad caught his balance and followed the officer.

They entered a low, long room and Brad instantly saw the barred door in the far wall, glimpsed the corridor. A man in cotton shirt and shapeless trousers, sandals on his feet, stood up from a bench against another wall. Swift Spanish filled the room as he and the officer spoke a moment, the younger man gesturing to Brad. The man moved slowly toward the grilled door, and then Brad saw the ring of keys hanging from a peg a few feet to the left of the portal.

The officer turned to Brad. "You will be held here, Señor Ranger."

"For how long?"

"*Quien sabe?* I shall send report by rider south. It will go to Mexico City. Your people will be informed. These things take time."

"I know. Point is, how much?"

"Months, perhaps."

The sandaled man had now unlocked the barred door and swung it open. On a brief order, one of the Rurales produced a key and unlocked Brad's manacles. The officer said, "Such as it is, you will have the best cell. Window looks out on the yard. There will be a breeze of sorts now and then. If you have money, the jailer will bring food from the cantina. Aquardiente, if you like."

"Well," Brad smiled wryly, "that's something, at least. But months!"

"It is too bad. But this is a thing between governments, you understand." The smile flashed again, this time friendly. "It might be, if you have pesos, the wait will not be lonely. The girls of Callita. . . ."

His lifted brow finished the sentence. Brad shook his head in a sardonic wonder. "I guess a Rurale jail is one to land in."

"The town's," the officer corrected. "But you are *our* prisoner. I have told the jailer to get whatever you wish to pay for. It is so little I can do for one who wears your badge. We have respect and liking for Rangers, señor."

Brad straightened slightly, touched his hat brim in a near-salute. "Thank you, Lieutenant. We have heard many stories of the Rurales."

The officer straightened, hand coming

smartly to his sombrero, dropping. He turned on his heel and walked out of the building. The jailer moved down a corridor from the door, and one of the Rurale troopers indicated Brad should follow.

Shortly after, another barred door closed on Brad and the key turned in the lock. Steps faded down the corridor, and there was only silence. Brad turned from the door, crossed the cell with its cot, two buckets in a corner, and walked to the window. He looked through bars across a bare, sandy yard on the sun-baked rear walls of adobes that might be houses or stores, he could not tell.

Glaring sun baked the yard but did not reach into the window. Brad noted the strong bars set firmly in the deep window, gave one of them a tug.

He dropped his hand, turned back to the cell. He took off his hat, dropped it on the floor, and sat down on the bunk. He looked around at the thick walls dividing his cell from the others, at barred window, and door. Then his head swiveled as he heard an approaching, shuffling sound in the corridor.

The jailer appeared, a man behind him. This was one Brad had not seen before, and he did not wear the Rurale uniform. But he held a Colt in his hand and stood back as the jailer unlocked the door and stepped into the cell. He spoke in rapid Spanish and Brad shook his head.

The man indicated the buckets, picked them up. Then he touched his mouth and moved his lips as though eating. He threw back his head as though he drank. He then extended his hand, thumb rubbing forefinger in the ancient symbol of the pay-off. Brad pulled out his purse, selected a silver coin, and tossed it to him.

The man's eyes lighted as he caught and examined it. He nodded, grinning, backed out of the cell and slammed the door. The key turned and jailer and guard disappeared.

Brad sank back on the bunk. At least, so long as money lasted, this would be comfortable. But it was jail. And Cochran rode free. And Brad would be here a long, long time. When word reached Tucson. . . .

Brad involuntarily shivered.

# Chapter Twelve

The long day and the longer night passed. Brad's money bought him as good food as could be had in Callita, but the Mexican way of cooking was too hot for his taste. Even the bottle of aquardiente held fire captive, and a sip or two proved enough.

Brad stretched out on the bunk in the pitch dark cell and heard faint sounds from the street. A guitar played somewhere, a ranchera. His mind followed it until, in some tripping musical phrase, he drifted off to sleep. He awakened as dawn streaked pale light through the bars.

When the jailer came in, this time without guard, confident of more money, Brad tried to ask about the Rurales by a series of signs. At last the man understood and made a wide sweeping movement toward the south and west. Brad caught only the name "Cochran!" and gathered that the pursuit for the outlaw had spread far in the direction the jailer indicated.

He ate well, and then there was nothing to do but lie on the bunk and watch the sky through the bars or stand at the window and look at the dull brown adobe walls far across the empty yard. He alternated these the whole day between fitful bits of sleep. Just before dusk he had the evening meal, and then the jailer left with the lantern.

Brad, surfeited with lying on the bunk and with rest, moved irritably around the cramped confines of the cell. Outside dark night reigned, alleviated only by the brilliant stars when he would stand at the window. He heard faint voices, laughter, the liquid run of soft Spanish. He mentally cursed his imprisonment and threw himself on the bunk again.

A few moments later, he stiffened. The faint sound did not come again and he finally told himself he had imagined it. He squirmed his shoulders and body to the contours of the bunk and closed his eyes. They snapped open again.

The sound — a soft sense, really, of movement beyond the window. He lay quite still, ears straining. It came again, almost as though it was under the window. Brad threw a glance at the dark cell corridor, swung his legs over the edge of the bunk, and eased to his feet. Three silent steps and he stood at the window. He looked out, saw only the gray uncertain shape of the yard, the velvet sky, and the bright stars.

He shifted his weight, and his body made a whisper against the adobe wall. He stiffened again, catching the rhythm of breathing, close. He moved to the edge of the window, thinking a man with a gun just outside would have an excellent target if Brad framed himself.

He breathed shallowly, ears straining for another sound. It came, a slight scraping, and then, slowly, he saw a break in the straight black line of the lower window. An indistinct shape became a darker shadow against the faint gray of the barren yard beyond the window. Brad's lips pressed in a thin, harsh line. Juan Cochran might be bold enough to set up an ambush even in a jail.

A whisper came, strained and hoarse. "Brad?"

Brad started, then caution held him. He waited. The indistinct form lifted, and Brad recognized the shape of a Stetson. The voice came again, strained. "Brad? You there?"

Brad flattened against the wall, back out of line with the window. "I'm here," he answered.

Now the shadow seemed to jump into frame in the barred window. He saw the shadowy shape of head and shoulders under the Stetson. Arms silhouetted against the faint gray beyond the window as the man grasped the bars with both hands. "It's Waco, Brad."

Brad at the same instant recognized the voice. He surged from the wall to the window. In the dim light, he caught the flash of Waco's grin. Brad's voice came in a relieved but wondering whisper. "How did you get here?"

"Saw they had you and saw them chase Manuel's bunch — or maybe Cochran's. So, figured you'd fallen right into the Rurales. Lucky, the *bandido* were so busy running from Rurales, they forgot about me. I made myself scarce from them and the Rurales, holed up until night. I figured Callita was the only place they could take you, so I rode in."

"What about Cochran?"

"I didn't hang around to find out. After the Rurales choused his boys around, I figure Juan will be suspicious of any stranger. No quicker way of getting killed than trying to say 'Howdy' at a time like that. Besides, Gregorio won't be exactly friendly, seeing I knocked him out of the saddle. So, I trailed here."

"How'd you find me?"

"How many saw the Rurales bring you in? The talk's all over town. I just had to listen. Only trouble was finding the right cell. When do you go up before the town *jefe*?"

Brad sighed. "Probably never. I've sort of twisted a treaty, I reckon. They'll probably take me to Mexico City for trial — when they get around to it."

Waco made a low, hopeless whistle. "They found your badge."

"They were looking for it. By the time everything's gone through all the government wheels on both sides of the border, I could add a year or two to my age."

Waco grunted thoughtfully. "Here, I figured you'd bail yourself out and we'd go for Cochran."

"Not a chance!" Brad suddenly looked back over his shoulder at the dark corridor. His voice dropped. "Where's the jailer?"

"Asleep in the front office. I made sure of him before I chanced hunting you from window to window."

"The Rurales?"

"Rode out before noon — most of 'em south with that young officer jasper. Four went north . . . regular border patrol, I reckon."

Brad hesitated then spoke flatly. "Waco, I'll give you a choice. No hard feelings however you decide."

"What kind of a choice?"

"You can slip away from Callita, get your Juan Cochran, and collect your reward if you want. If you don't, you can head right back across the border to Piedra Mala. Or — you can run the risk of more trouble down here helping me break out."

"What kind of a choice is that!"

Brad answered dryly, "Big enough. Safety, and you won't have to pay me part of Cochran's reward. Or you'll be right in here with me, to name the risk, and for a long time."

"The way things stand, I don't get Cochran without your help now that he's stirred up and suspicious." The laughter suddenly left Waco's voice. "Maybe it's my fault you've read me wrong, Nolan. You took my offer. That makes you my partner. Even if I could get Cochran by myself, I don't sell a partner short. I like money — but not that much. Now . . . how do we get you out?"

Brad felt a surge of warmth for this man who claimed only money talked for him. He heard Waco test the bars. "Not a chance. They're firm and deep. Not even a rope and a horse would move 'em. And that's another problem — a horse for me."

"Spotted yours in a corral just over there."

Brad again considered the dark corridor. "You know the jailer? the old man?"

"Sure."

"I'm going to call him and send him to the cantina for tequila or something. You can handle it from there?"

Waco's answer was a chuckle and his shadow suddenly disappeared. Brad heard the faint whisper of his steps as he eased toward the front of the building. Brad crossed the dark cell to the door, picked up one of the buckets beside it, and banged on the bars. The sound boomed and echoed down the corridor.

In a moment, a light flickered, grew steady, and a querulous voice called, *"Quien es?"*

"Aguardiente, *por favor*!"

*"Si!"*

The light brightened as the man came hurrying down the corridor. He stopped, lantern held high in one hand, the other extended for coins. Brad fished them from his pocket and dropped them in the dark palm. He gestured to himself, then to the jailer. The man grinned, bobbed his head, and hurried away.

The light swiftly faded, leaving cell and

passageway in darkness. Brad remained by the door, grasping the bars, listening. But he heard no more than the usual distant, faint sounds from the street. It seemed that time dragged.

He stiffened, cheeks pressed against the bars. He had heard a sound, one that he couldn't distinguish. There were other sounds, something dragging, a glow of light, A door clanged, and then the light brightened toward him.

Waco appeared, carrying lantern and the ring of keys. Brad's explosive grin matched his. Waco inserted the key in the lock, turned it, swung open the door.

"The old man?" Brad asked.

"Locked in one of his own cells. He'll wake up with a knot on his head." Waco's smile widened. "But he'll have a full two bottles of whisky beside him. I don't reckon he'll raise too much hell until he's slept off his drunk."

Brad stepped into the corridor. "Horses?"

"First thing," Waco indicated Brad's empty holster, "is your gun. Stay back here while I look around in the office."

Brad hurried with him to the barred corridor door, swinging open. Waco, carrying the lantern, walked on into the office and now Brad saw the street door had been closed. He heard Waco moving around, some kind of door open. A moment later, the bounty hunter appeared holding both Brad's Colt and rifle. He thrust them at Brad. "All but the badge, Ranger."

"They've sent that to Mexico City as evidence."

"May it do 'em some good." Waco grew serious. "From now until we ride out. . . ."

Brad nodded, checked his gun, and nodded toward the door. "Blow out the lantern and let's get on saddle leather."

A moment later, Waco eased the planked door back, almost inch by inch. Gradually the Stygian darkness of the office lessened, and Brad saw a part of Waco's body outlined in the open space between door and jamb. A moment's pause and then Waco's hiss, "It'll never be no better. Cut left around the building after me."

Brad touched his shoulder in acknowledgment and Waco slid through the aperture. Brad followed. He had a glimpse of a dark street, relieved here and there by the subdued glow of lamps or candlelight from buildings across the plaza. He whipped around the corner of the building as he made out the dim shapes of two riders lazying in this direction. A second later, Waco moved close behind him and they both flattened against the wall. The two riders passed by and the slow-paced sound of their passages continued and finally faded.

Waco said, "I'll lead."

He moved around Brad, who followed him onto the rear of the jail. They swiftly angled across the barren ground Brad had so often seen from his window. Shortly, he saw the indistinct shape of a corral beyond. Waco circled it, swung open a gate. Brad saw the dark shape of a horse, gave a low whistle, and the animal came trotting forward.

Waco suddenly swore under his breath. "Bridle and saddle! They're probably in the jail. Hang and rattle. I'll get 'em."

He was gone. Brad remained in the corral, the bay nuzzling him now and then. Brad saw no light come on in the jail, but those scattered along the plaza seemed threatening rather than warm. Once he heard a distant shout and he instantly froze. But the sound was not repeated, nor was there any sign of alarm.

Suddenly Waco reappeared, saddle on his shoulder, bridle reins trailing from his hand. He dumped them on the ground with a relieved sigh. "They had 'em in a cell for safekeeping. Took the devil's own time to find 'em."

"No trouble?" Brad swung the saddle up

and turned to the bay.

"None. Our friend's still sleeping tight. I must've leaned harder on that gun barrel than I thought. He's going to need that firewater bad when he comes around."

Brad moved with swift efficiency, fingers nimble and sure even in the dark. Waco watched toward the street. When Brad was ready, the bounty hunter motioned back toward the silent, dark adobes. "My horse is over there. Best lead yours until we're ready to rattle out."

They moved silently across the yard, keeping close attention to the jail and the town. But nothing moved along the plaza, there was no shout from the jail. Ahead of them, something stirred, and then Brad saw Waco's saddled horse. The bounty hunter spoke a low word, picked up the reins that ground-tied the animal. He and Brad swung into their saddles simultaneously. Waco neck-reined his mount toward the adobes and Brad followed.

They moved the length of the structures, and Waco turned into a narrow lane that led between small shacks. Brad, looking back over his shoulder, saw the distant lamplight from buildings on the plaza. He swung around, startled, hand dropping to his gun, when a dog suddenly barked savagely near by.

Waco's voice drifted back. "No trouble. The town's used to riders in the night. Juan Cochran trained it."

The dog's barking slowly faded behind them. No lights came on, and no one seemed to be curious. Gradually Brad's hand moved away from the gun. At long last, the final buildings faded behind them and Brad judged, by the stars, they headed due west. Waco kept to the course until well out of Callita, then he turned northward and angled east.

He spoke when Brad came up beside him. "We're heading back to the main road leading to the border. We'll cross it and then parallel it maybe a hundred yards beyond, just in case Rurales or *bandido* happen to be around."

Brad eased into the saddle, setting himself for the long ride. In a short time, they came on the road, a broad gray band in the darkness. They drew rein, listening, casting their eyes south toward the distant town, invisible now, and then north. So far as they could tell, they were the only things alive in this silent, star-strewn universe. A moment later, they crossed the road and, well out, turned northward to follow it.

Brad knew there were comparatively few

miles to the border, but they seemed to stretch out and out. Now and then they stopped to strain sight and hearing ahead. They moved slowly for fear of running blindly onto a night camp of Rurales or outlaws. Time, like the miles, passed with torturous slowness.

Waco finally drew rein, twisted around in the saddle to face Brad. "We're close to the border, I figure. If the Rurales are anywhere, it'll be around here."

Brad lifted the reins. "I'd figure it. If they do jump us, best to just cut and run."

"And straight ahead. Arizona can't be more'n a mile, if that."

They moved forward, even more slowly now. It seemed to Brad that each brush and cactus held a threat, its dark shape fading behind them with infinite slowness. Their horses' hoofs made only little shuffle-whispers, but that sounded like thunder to the two tense and cautious men.

Suddenly Brad straightened, pointed ahead. "Piedra Mala?"

Faint lights twinkled uncertainly far ahead. Waco studied them a moment, spoke aloud for the first time and with a gusting of breath. "Sure as hell! We've made it!"

# Chapter Thirteen

Piedra Mala did not fully represent safety, and the two men knew it. What with the Rurales around the village and Callita, Juan Cochran and his band could have fled northward to this comparative safety. So, though relieved to pass the first dark house, they still rode cautiously toward the hanging lantern before the livery stable. Their eyes cast toward the faint glow of light from the saloon and that streaming out the open door of the hotel.

Even as they watched and rode toward it, the lamps in the saloon snapped out. Piedra Mala had officially ended another of its evil days. Now Brad rode more confidently, angling toward the stable.

Not long after, they left the empty, silent street, strode across the hotel porch, and entered the lobby. The lamp burned over the counter, revealing empty, cracked leather chairs. A door behind the counter stood partially opened. They had taken but few strides toward the stairway leading to the upper rooms, when the door swung wide and the fat proprietor stood framed.

His wide yawn snapped off as he saw them, and his eyes widened in their folds of flesh. "Thought you gents had gone."

Waco said shortly, "Did we give up our rooms?"

"No, just heard that —"

"Where?" Brad cut in tightly. "Who?"

"Why, I dunno. Someone saw you two ride out. Talk had it you wouldn't be back. Heard that maybe a dozen times. Can't say who started it."

Brad sighed. "Surprising how wild guesses get to be truth. Did you rent our rooms?"

The man made a weary, wry grin. "Who to? Had anyone come in since you left, I had plenty of places to put 'em. Not that anyone did."

Brad nodded and the sharpness left his voice. "Then we'll turn in. Goodnight."

" 'Night."

Brad knew that the fat man curiously watched after them as they climbed the stairs. Brad led the way to his own room, entered, Waco groping behind him. Brad pulled the shade on the window facing the street, stepped aside, and then lit a match.

He applied it to the lampwick and looked swiftly around. The boxlike area looked exactly as he had left it.

He sailed his hat on the bed where Waco sat, unbuckled his gunbelt. "We're lucky."

"That's certain," Waco sighed and yawned. "A lot of riding for nothing."

"Figured why?"

Waco looked up, ran his fingers through his shock of red hair. "Sure, Gregorio spotted you as the Ranger who killed Louis Cardonez. And then the Rurales . . . just bad luck."

"That it was, but planned."

Waco eyed him levelly, and Brad could see the dawning comprehension. Brad pointed to the floor. "Our friend downstairs — he said we were seen riding out. We went separately and met outside town. Let me ask you, why did Gregorio show up at crack of dawn down there? And, if he wasn't right here in Piedra Mala, how did he know who I was?"

Waco grunted. "And the Rurales showing up, a whole troop of them."

"Almost right on time," Brad drove it home, "like they were looking for us — or Cochran — or both. How did they know to ride that direction — just then?"

"Someone had to tell them. Who?"

Brad stood up, started unbuttoning his shirt. "It's a guess and nothing more. But I'd first say Dean Harris."

"The manager!"

"Himself."

"But — he was robbed. He called in the law. He's the one who lost gold and money."

Brad grinned tightly and jerked his thumb toward the door. "I'm too tired to sit around guessing the rest of the night. But you can take this to your room to gnaw on before you go to sleep. It wasn't Dean Harris' gold and money that was stolen."

"Then whose?"

"The Golden Eagle Mine — a corporation, owners back east somewhere."

Waco's eyes rounded, and his lips formed a soundless whistle. Then his brows knitted down, and he shook his head. "You've swung a mighty wide loop there."

"Too wide to argue about tonight. How about morning?"

Waco pulled himself from the bed and moved slowly to the door. He turned. "Like you said, something to gnaw on. Now here's something for you. Cochran's still loose, and a peso gets you a dollar he's on the prowl for you. Keep your gun handy."

Brad nodded, and Waco went out in the hall. Brad closed and locked the door behind him, blew out the lamp. He then lifted the blind, grateful for the warm night breeze that blew in. He slowly undressed, eyes thoughtful on the dark street below. Fully undressed, he turned again to the window and searched far into the darkness toward Mexico. He had a swift, graphic picture of a young Rurale officer down there somewhere, heading toward Mexico City with a Ranger badge as evidence.

Brad's lips twisted, half worry and half sardonic. There'd be a lot of explaining to do in Callita about a bird flown from the coop. But there might also be a lot of explaining to do in Tucson about a Ranger badge. Brad shrugged. Leave that worry to its proper time and place. He dropped onto the bed and, almost in a matter of seconds, he fell asleep, his fingers touching the metal of the Colt between his pillow and the wall.

He slept late, and the busy sounds from the street below awakened him. He sat up, yawning, looked about the room with a pleasure its ugliness did not warrant. But it was so much more beautiful than a jail cell! He grinned at the thought, swung out of bed, and prepared for the day.

Shaved and dressed, he buckled on his gunbelt and adjusted the holster to his leg. He looked out on the street, already sun baking, and his gaze moved to the café across the street. His eyes lighted and he hurriedly grabbed up his Stetson, brushed dust from it, and turned to the door.

Brad came out on the roofed porch, swiftly crossed it, and stopped short at the head of the steps. Hank Lewis looked up at him, dark eyes wide in surprise. The marshal caught himself, and his thin lips twisted in a travesty of a greeting. "Morning, Ranger. Heard you'd left for good. Too bad it ain't so."

Brad ignored the spurring. "Where'd you hear it?"

"Well, now, can't really say. Maybe it was something in the wind."

"Or one of Cochran's sidekicks?"

Lewis' smile widened in almost direct challenge. "That might be. We get along."

"Too well."

The marshal scowled. "It's my town."

"So far."

Brad walked off, leaving the marshal fuming. He crossed the street and entered the café. The breakfast business had long been finished and it was that lull before the noon meal. Mary Alma appeared at the tinkle of the bell. She saw Brad, hastily hid a glad surprise. "I didn't expect to see you."

He sat down at one of the tables. "No one

did. What kind of word got around?"

"That you'd left."

Brad sighed. "I've been asking but getting no answer. Maybe you know. Who said I rode out for good?"

"I don't know." She added hastily when Brad's face fell. "I heard Manse Joad say he heard it from Hank Lewis."

"The marshal."

"Well, maybe he heard it from someone else. Things get spread around, and no one really knows how they start."

Brad shrugged, smiled. "That's for sure. Right now, I'd rather have breakfast than worry about it."

"That's easy come by."

She smiled and went into the kitchen. Brad rested his elbows on the table, listening to the sounds she made beyond the doorway. Hank Lewis, he thought, and it didn't surprise him. Point was now, had Hank been told by someone else or had he direct knowledge? Brad frowned, inclined to feel Hank had heard it. The other way made a crooked lawman of him, something not to be considered until it was forced upon you.

Mary came with his breakfast. He hoped that she would have coffee with him as she had done before. But she only served him, murmured a hurried excuse, and returned to the kitchen. He heard her giving orders to the Indian woman, heard the clatter of a stove lid. He sighed, disappointed, and then turned hungrily to the eggs and ham and coffee.

The tinkle of the doorbell brought Brad wheeling about in his chair. Waco Mead entered, lifted a hand in greeting. At that moment, Mary again appeared. Waco dropped into a chair at Brad's table, spoke a friendly word to Mary, and ordered. She left them, and Brad gave close attention to the remainder of his breakfast. His ears had been all too keen to detect the familiarity in Waco's voice and her reply.

Waco had not noticed. "Still figuring like you did last night?"

"There's been nothing to change my mind. Seems like our marshal knew a lot about it, too."

"Crooked!"

"Maybe."

They broke off when Mary returned with Waco's breakfast. The bounty hunter grinned widely at her and Brad saw the answering faint smile. He felt a twinge of anger and then choked it down. He had no right to feel anything, one way or the other, about Mary Alma, what she did or whom she liked. He felt confusion at the new and strange emotions that stirred within him.

Mary left them again, and Waco tackled his food. He spoke between mouthfuls. "I been thinking about what you said. One way it makes sense, another way it don't. Say it does, how are you going to prove it?"

Brad frowned. "If Harris is crooked, there'll be nothing we can turn up in Piedra Mala. He'd be a fool to chance the gossip that goes on."

Waco worked on an egg. "Where's Cochran figure? He's the gent I want, no matter how Harris is tangled up in it. There's no reward on him."

Brad leaned back in his chair, absently moving his coffee mug around on the table. "We've got Juan Cochran, an outlaw and his gang working both sides of the border. We got Hank Lewis, a marshal who looks the other way when the outlaw comes to town. We got Dean Harris, who's robbed by the outlaw, but wants to call the whole thing off when the sheriff calls in a Ranger."

"Keep thinking out loud," Waco prompted.

"When you and me go over the border, word has been sent ahead. I figure it was done by either Harris or Hank Lewis, but I'd give the edge to Harris."

"You keep looking his way, but how are you going to brand him?"

"Cochise Springs, maybe. He makes a lot of trips there, I hear. Says he can have a better time there than in Piedra Mala, and the girls are more friendly. But maybe there's something else he likes."

"Such as?"

"A bank, maybe — or high stakes gambling — or a Wells Fargo station that'll take shipments of one kind or another." Brad swallowed the last of his coffee. "I think I'll look around up there."

Waco sighed. "And this'd be the time for it. Cochran's bound to stay clear out of sight until he's sure the Rurales are gone. Word will be around you broke out of Callita, so he'll know you're up here and waiting."

Brad decided, "I'll ride out tomorrow. Be back in a few days."

They had both finished. Waco rapped on the table and Mary Alma appeared. They paid her, Waco boldly eyeing her as he counted coins and made mild jokes. She thanked them, and they walked out into the street. As they crossed to the hotel, Waco said, "Now there's a damn' pretty woman back there. I hear she's a widow. Now that's something to interest a man, ain't it?"

"I reckon."

Something in Brad's tone made Waco look sharply at him, then grin. "Well, what do you know! Looks like I'll have to move fast to beat a Ranger!"

Brad smiled, a faint move of the lips.

The day passed in hot monotony. Waco spent the time in the saloon at a desultory poker game. Brad had a drink, watched the game a while, and then went to the hotel. He watched the slow moving life of the town from the veranda. Late afternoon, he went up to his room, washed, shaved again, and critically inspected himself in the wavy mirror. That done, he swiftly returned to the street. He threw a hurried look at the saloon, but did not see Waco. A moment later, he entered the café.

Mary Alma had time only to speak a word, give him a smile, and take his order. Brad looked around at the diners at the other tables and mentally cursed their presence. Now and then he glanced toward the door, half expecting Waco but hoping the man wouldn't appear. The food Mary Alma served was excellent, but this time Brad was hardly aware of it. He ate slowly, hoping he would outlast the others, but it seemed that when a diner did leave, another came in to take his place. Defeated, Brad finally paid and left.

He returned to the hotel porch and joined the fat man. The proprietor made comments about passing people and riders as the twilight deepened. Brad answered with grunts, nods, an occasional word. He involuntarily straightened when he saw Waco emerge from the saloon, walk to the café, and go inside. Brad had to fight down the impulse to go over there himself. It seemed an eternity before Waco came out. He sauntered to the hotel, dropped into the chair beside Brad.

Night seeped into the town, and the lamps came on up and down the street. Waco finally arose, stretched. "How about a drink or a hand of poker?"

"Not tonight. I like it here."

"You've turned into the sittin'est man!" Waco commented, and sauntered off.

Half an hour later, Brad saw the café go dark. He instantly arose, spoke a casual word to his fat companion, and stepped down onto the street. He angled across it and was but a step away when Mary Alma turned from locking the door. "Mr. Nolan!"

"Evening." He rushed on, "Going home?"

"Yes, I am."

"It's mighty dark."

"It generally is. I'm used to it."

"Still and all —"

She cut in, kind but determined. "I appreciate your thought, Mr. Nolan, but I'm quite safe. Good night."

She smiled and he could do nothing but repeat "Goodnight" and step aside, his face flaming in the dark. She moved on and away from him. Brad finally replaced his hat, and then swung around when he heard a low snicker.

Waco Mead leaned against the front of the store between the café and the saloon. "Next time handcuff her, Ranger. Now, how about that drink? It ain't a lucky day for either of us."

# Chapter Fourteen

The next day, Brad reluctantly rode out of Piedra Mala. Now that Waco had become aware of Mary Alma and there was an unspoken rivalry between him and Brad, the plan to go to Cochise Springs seemed ill-timed. But Brad could think of no excuse to defer it, except Mary Alma, and he didn't dare mention that.

He passed through the town where the tip had sent him stumbling onto Waco Mead instead of Juan Cochran. Night found him well beyond, but Cochise Springs still many hours ahead. He made a camp and tried to rest. But his mind kept bringing up visions of Waco Mead back in Piedra Mala. He'd be talking to Mary Alma now. Maybe tonight, he'd walk her home, where Brad had failed last night. Brad stared into the dying embers of his small fire. He kept seeing her face, the smoke-violet eyes, the shape of her lips when she smiled.

Finally, he kicked sand over the embers and stretched out on his blanket, his saddle his pillow. He stared up at the stars and spoke aloud. "You've found her, Brad Nolan. It wasn't Joanie or any of them before her. It's Mary Alma."

He sat up, hugging his knees, frowning toward the low black blobs of desert plants, a gaunt silhouette of an angular saguaro. His mind seemed to speak aloud to him. "She likes you, but not like that. She's had too much with her husband. She wants something safe, a man who's got a chance of making something of himself."

He hugged his knees tighter, a half hopeless reaction to his thoughts. "No law badge and gun-fighting man for her! Don't blame her. Where does that leave you? Nowhere!"

He absently scuffed at sand with his boot heel. He realized he faced a time of decision more clear cut than with Waco, though one thing was tied in with the other. He had enough self assurance that he might stand a chance with Mary Alma if he was not a Ranger, if he had something to offer. Like now, riding off to some town to get evidence to support or destroy a suspicion about a man. It would be like that, and she'd know it, so long as he upheld the law. So. . . .

He sat quite still, eyes narrowed as his mind came down to the basic choice. As a Ranger he had no chance at all to win this woman who, perhaps unknown to herself, had come into his life and taken his heart. Without the law badge, he had a chance, however slim. But not as a drifter. Brad eased back on the blanket.

So be it, then! Wind up this whole business of Juan Cochran, including this trip to Cochise Springs. Get back to Piedra Mala as soon as Harris was cleared or his guilt confirmed. Throw in with Waco, get a share of the reward, and then, the assignment completed, resign from the Rangers. Go after Mary Alma.

The sense of firm decision remained with Brad the next morning when he awoke. He had a skimpy breakfast, smothered his small fire, and was soon in the saddle. By late morning, he rode into Cochise Springs, a busy ranching and mining town strung for a mile or more along the winding course of a deep gulch. He saw many stores, saloons, and the narrow, crooked main street was filled with ore and ranch wagons, riders and people scurrying in and out of the stores.

He came on the railroad station, a dull brown structure at the end of tracks down from the north. Brad went to the telegraph office and spent a painful time partially writing and tearing up telegrams. Finally, he handed a yellow blank to the telegrapher, who read it back to him in an impersonal voice.

"Rangers — Tucson. Assignment may lead to inside job. Am checking Cochise Springs." The man looked up sharply at Brad before he continued. "Badge taken south Piedra Mala. Send another or letter authority Cochise Springs. Also any information earnings mine last year or two. Nolan."

Brad paid for the wire, watched the man turn to the key and start pounding out the message. Then Brad left and, outside, looked down the canyon on the stores, the adobes, houses, and shacks that seemed veritably to cling to the steep wall. He wondered what the Captain would say about the badge, and Brad felt a touch of guilt that he dismissed. He had told the truth, for that matter, and he hoped to wind this whole thing up before anything would come from Mexico City. By then, he'd be out of the Rangers — with luck.

He squared his shoulders and swung into the saddle, riding back down the canyon into the heart of the town. He rode slowly, eyes busy. He saw the bank and, just beyond, the Wells Fargo office. He hesitated, then rode on, saving them for the time when he could show definite authority. He considered two or three saloons, passed them by as a waste of time.

Then, just ahead, he saw one that offered possibilities. It looked more prosperous than the others, less garish. The sign read "Ranchers' Rest," dull golden letters on a black background. Brad turned in to the rail, dismounted. As he tied his horse, he glanced at the few others. They were not the mounts that the average cowboy would use out on the range. Their owners had paid considerable money for them.

Brad went into the saloon. In many ways it was typical, but Brad instantly noticed the bar had a dull waxen gleam and the brass spittoons were bright and polished. The tables, scattered spaciously about the big room were large, well kept, and also polished. Each had three or four comfortable chairs. The Ranchers' Rest, Brad saw, accented comfort and ease rather than noise and crowds. In a far corner, three well-dressed men sat at a card game, bottles and glasses at their hands. A Mexican, neatly dressed, sat nearby in a chair at the wall, ready to serve instantly.

Brad walked on to the bar. The man

behind it wore a gleaming white shirt and black string tie. He studied Brad with polite appraisal, his expression neither welcoming nor rejecting. He came up as Brad reached the bar.

"Howdy," the man said in an impersonal tone. His eyes flicked to the dust stains on Brad's shirt and hat. "You just rode in?"

"That's right — and I'm thirsty."

"Figures — but most punchers figure our prices are too high. You're range riding?"

Brad smiled slightly. "I'm not a hired hand, if that bothers you. I picked the place because it looks my style, and I've heard of it."

"Who told you?"

"Dean Harris, down in Piedra Mala."

The bartender's impersonal air vanished. He smiled and then apologized, "Sorry to ask your brand, but we don't want drifters off the street. Now what's your drink?"

Brad ordered. The bartender left him to whisky and glass, moving down the bar. Brad listened to the subdued voices from the card game, an occasional lifting laugh. He noted the little marks of luxury, the framed mirrors, the waxed floor devoid of the usual sawdust. The place spoke of the richness in the Cochise Springs area and of the men who had that wealth. Perhaps, Brad thought, Dean Harris was one of the class that came here, but the place seemed more for ranch and mine owners rather than foremen and managers. He filled his shot glass again and caught the bartender's eye.

The man came to him, brow lifted in question. Brad leaned toward him. "I'm a stranger, like you guessed. But Dean said some fun could be had if a man knew who to ask."

"Cards?" the bartender asked. "Come tonight. That's a private game over there."

"Well, a little more'n cards."

A faint, knowing smile touched the bartender's lips. "I think Mr. Harris thought of the Rosita Adobe. Down the street four blocks and turn left. Climb the hill and you'll see it. Sits all to itself. Mention Mr. Harris or —" the man smiled affably "— me, Joe Cahern. Rosita will make you welcome."

"It's all right?"

"The best — and the girls are refined."

A few moments later, Brad left the Ranchers' Rest. He swung into saddle, rode off in the direction the bartender had suggested. But at the next block he turned off up a steep street, found the next that seemed to cling to a ledge of the lower canyon wall, and retraced his way back toward the telegraph station.

Ranchers' Rest and Rosita's, he thought. The saloon catered only to the wealthy or near-wealthy, as he had seen. Rosita probably had the same exclusive clientele, men who would spend a good deal of money on the girls. Brad's lips pursed — saloon or house, either seemed out of the class of the mine manager. Brad's eyes faintly lighted. It looked as though his suspicion would be confirmed.

The telegrapher looked up as Brad entered. Just then the key started chattering and the man turned to it. He spoke hurriedly as his pencil followed the clicking key. "For you — Tucson."

Brad listened eagerly to the incomprehensible chatter of the key. It stopped momentarily and the telegrapher tore off the sheet from the pad. Then the key started again and once more the pencil flew. At last the man stood up as the key went silent and turned to the counter.

"Both for you. This'n first."

Brad read the scrawl on the yellow sheet. "Continue check Cochise Springs. But main assignment JC. Will send mine statement earnings when received. Have wired Chicago. Authority follows wire. Expect explanation lost badge with final report assignment. New badge Piedra Mala stage. Identify and pick up. This week. Expect wind-up case shortly."

Brad grimaced at the implications, then swiftly read the second wire. It stated tersely that Brad Nolan was an Arizona Ranger with all authorities and powers. On identification, Brad was to be accorded all co-operation due a Territorial law officer.

Brad folded both sheets, thanked the telegrapher who looked at him with new respect. Brad returned to the town and dismounted before the bank. He went inside and soon talked to a portly, sideburned man in a private office. When Brad came out on the street again, he frowned, now not too sure that his guess had been right.

The banker knew Dean Harris, right enough. But Harris had made no large deposits, none that could not be explained by his salary. The banker admitted they handled the Golden Eagle account, accepting gold ore and transmitting its value to a San Francisco bank that handled the corporate account. Brad had found nothing suspicious here, unless he counted the banker's statement that in the last three years, ore from the mine had decreased steadily. But that could be explained by dwindling veins of the metal.

Brad went to Wells Fargo. He was again questioned sharply to confirm his identity, and then the manager agreed to answer questions. At first, Brad thought he had failed again. There was no record of any shipments from either Golden Eagle or Dean Harris. Brad felt his expectations explode. He sighed and stood up, thanking the man.

Some impulse made him ask, "Then you've had no shipments of money or gold from Piedra Mala?"

"I didn't say that, Mr. Nolan. We've had none from Dean Harris or a Golden Eagle Mine."

Brad's hopes came to sudden life. "But gold-dust shipments?"

"Yes — over the past three years."

"By who?"

"A man named Orin."

"Orin!" Brad recalled the murdered superintendent.

"That's right. I gather he has a strike down there and he's managed to keep it quiet. If you didn't have the authority, I wouldn't be telling you this. But Orin has made steady deposits, and we've sent drafts covering it to a Los Angeles bank."

"Orin?" Brad scratched his head. This didn't fit with the picture he had so far.

"Have you met him?"

"Oh, yes. He's about your height but dark — hair and eyes. Wears black — shirt, trousers, hat, and boots. I'd never guess him to be a miner, but he has come regularly almost every month."

"Since the robbery at Golden Eagle?"

"That Juan Cochran raid?" The man suddenly frowned. "Come to think of it, he hasn't. Is there any connection?"

"Now I wouldn't know," Brad said softly, "but I aim to find out. Could I see those receipts?"

Brad rode out of Cochise Springs surprised by what he had learned, but satisfied. A few questions around Piedra Mala and he'd make some unexpected arrests. One of them, he thought, would be a pleasure.

He arrived in Piedra Mala the following day just at dusk. The town looked as dead and scabrous as ever. He dismounted, weary and hungry, at the livery stable, started to the hotel, but the gnawing of an empty stomach changed his mind. He abruptly changed his course and entered the café.

The supper trade was over, and the small room was empty. He heard the rattle of dishes beyond the far wall and then Mary came through the doorway, answering the tinkle of the bell. She involuntarily stopped short when she saw Brad, and the lamplight disclosed the sudden glad light in her eyes and the instant warm flash of her smile.

She swept forward as Brad stood hat in hand, clothing dust-stained with the long miles south. She caught herself up, and her pace slowed. He saw the faint darker color in her neck and cheeks, and then she composed her features to a more sedate welcome.

"Mr. Nolan! Welcome back. I . . . we though you might have left us for good."

Brad sank into the chair, grinning. He suddenly knew that she had missed him and that there was a more than casual friendship here. It was beyond logic, but he knew.

He suddenly realized that his amazing thoughts must be mirrored in his face, in his eyes. Mary looked confused, uncertain, and embarrassed. He covered his own swirling emotions with, "I reckon I'm too late for supper?"

"Oh, no. We're cleaning up, but there's food. You're the last for the day. What'll you have?"

"What's handy."

She started to turn but he blurted, "Mary!"

She checked, slowly turned. "Yes?"

"You're closing up? . . . after . . . ?"
"Yes?"
He looked toward the window. "It's coming full dark. Maybe I could . . . ?"
She hesitated and then her smile surrendered. "It would be nice."
She fled to the kitchen.

# Chapter Fifteen

The fat man, lolling in a chair on the dark hotel porch, looked up when he heard the whistling. A moment later, Brad came up the steps, the lamplight from the open doorway falling full on him. The fat man pulled himself around. "Now that's what this town needs — whistling. Easy whistling, that is, not the kind you do walking by a graveyard."

Brad laughed. "Ever tried it?"

"Nothing to whistle about."

"I'd say you've never looked at your own town."

"Hard and often. That's why I can't whistle."

Brad waved a careless hand at him, crossed the porch, and went inside. The moment he stepped into his own room, the trapped heat struck him almost like a blow. He crossed and opened the window, lit the lamp, and swiftly peeled out of his shirt. He heard a tap on the door and he whirled about, stepped to his gunbelt on the bed, and drew the Colt. Then he opened the door.

Waco Mead stepped in, saw the gun, and looked sharply at Brad. "Not that I blame you, but looks like you're jumpy."

Brad closed the door. "The more I find out, the more reason."

He circled Waco, ignoring the question in the man's eyes, and holstered his gun. He mopped sweat from his face, waved Waco to the bed, and then lifted the window blind. A second later, he blew out the lamp. "They must build in the heat with the rest of it."

Waco's blocky shape was half-defined in the shadows. "Saw you ride in and go to Mary's."

"Supper, and damn' famished."

"And walked her home?"

Brad caught the sharp edge in the man's voice. He asked quietly, "Does it bother you, Waco?"

"Say I'm surprised. I've been working up a friendly with her — you know, joshing in the café when she comes up. But I never got to walking her home."

The edge was still there and Brad tried to dismiss it. "Just so-happen tonight. Has Juan Cochran made a move?"

"Not him — but I've seen a couple of gents that could be riding with him. They've been hanging around, off and on. First you see 'em, and then you don't."

"Looking for us?"

"Sure thing, not for me. Maybe trying to get a line on where you are. After all, you're the Ranger."

"But nothing about Cochran himself?"

"No sign, no move. What'd you find in Cochise Springs?"

"Enough to bring me scooting back here, fast. For instance, a man named Orin made regular gold-dust deposits with Wells Fargo, and they gave drafts to cover on a Los Angeles bank, mailing 'em there for Orin."

"The superintendent!"

"Same name. But the man in Cochise Springs named Orin was dark. I learned tonight Superintendent Orin had yellow hair and blue eyes."

Waco made a clucking sound in the darkness, asked abruptly, "Dean Harris?"

"Nothing direct. But he liked expensive things — the best saloons and the best girls. Neither of them come cheap up there."

"Mmmm . . . well, that's Harris and someone else. I'll stick with Juan Cochran where the money is."

"You couldn't move here anyway. For

once, the Ranger badge is worth something."

"Dinero?"

"No — but it can flush Cochran out and that means dinero. Our deal's still on?"

"I don't renege," Waco snapped stiffly.

"So I figured." Brad laughed grimly in the darkness. "Come tomorrow, we'll start earning that reward. I'm going to talk to two people — just talk this time. But you be ready for Cochran — or any other kind of hell. I'm sure it'll break."

"Can you tell me what it is?"

"I'd rather not. I'm certain in my own mind, but a lawman can go mighty wrong until he's proved things out. Or stirred 'em up enough, things start happening."

"Just so Cochran ends up in our hands."

"Get ready to split that reward," Brad said with a harsh laugh. "But right now, I want a bed and shut-eye."

Waco stood up and moved to the door. He stopped there and half turned. "Our deal stands. There's something else."

"What?"

"Mary Alma. I got ideas about her."

"So have I — like getting married."

"Man! You're real tangled up in a strong rope! Mean it?"

"I do."

"Well . . . we'll see."

He was gone and the door closed on the dark room before Brad could answer. His steps faded down the hall. Brad slowly turned to the window and looked out on the street. He heard a burst of laughter from the saloon but his eyes remained on the dark café.

He sighed, deeply, and then started undressing. He glanced at the dark door, seeing Waco again. He smiled with tight assurance. "That's right, friend — we'll see."

After breakfast, a meal whose savor was increased by what Brad believed he read in Mary's smile, an accidental touch of her hand, Brad crossed the street to the marshal's office. He looked in the door, saw Hank Lewis with the parts of a rifle scattered over his desk, oil and cleaning rag in his hand.

Lewis looked up with a disdainful gleam in his dark eyes. "Working or visiting, Ranger?"

"Working."

Brad entered and dropped into a chair without invitation. Lewis started to protest, thought better of it, and concentrated on the oily part in his hand. Brad waited and Lewis became increasingly uncertain. Now and then he'd throw covert, underbrow looks, and his hands moved faster with oil and rag. Finally, he asked, "What's your business?"

"What do you know about the mine superintendent who was killed in Callita?"

"Orin? Just knew him."

"And what about the knifing?"

The marshal looked up. "No more'n what anybody's heard. He fooled around with a woman and got some steel between his ribs for his trouble."

"Because of the woman — nothing else?"

Lewis sat quite still, dark eyes probing, jumping slightly from side to side. His thin lips finally curled. "Ranger, fool around with a Mex woman down there and see what happens!"

"I didn't ask that."

Lewis dropped the piece. "Maybe you'd better mark out your trail?"

"Orin was fair? blue-eyed?"

"Yes. What of it?"

"Did he ride around much?"

Lewis sighed in exasperation. "How would I know! From the mine here, down to Callita. That's it, so far as I know."

"Never to Cochise Springs?"

Lewis still held his angry pose but Brad detected a sudden, uncertain flicker in his eyes. He made an irritable gesture. "Ranger, you're touched with the sun or wasting my time. Either way, go somewhere else and ask your questions."

"Oh, I will," Brad pleasantly agreed. "Do you know of an Orin up that way?"

"Why in blazing hell should I!"

"I heard of one," Brad stood up. "Come up there regular, I learned. Said he came from Piedra Mala."

"Then it was Orin."

"But this one, I hear, is dark and wears dark clothes. They say he has a mine around here — one he works himself. Heard of him?"

Brad mentally gave the man credit for a great deal of control. For an instant, his jaw dropped and he blinked. Then he thrust out his jaw. "I never heard of anyone like that — let alone one named Orin."

Brad walked to the door. "I'd hoped you might. Now I have to look for him. Thanks for the help, marshal."

He walked out, moved lazily to the hotel, and entered the lobby. He stopped there and eased down into one of the worn leather chairs. The fat man came through a rear door, saw him. "This ain't no place to sit. Regular damn' oven. Come out on the porch."

"In a minute."

The fat man shook his head and went outside. Brad, feeling moisture gather on his face and on his body under his clothes, waited, watching the street through the dusty window. Time passed and Brad wondered if he had chosen the right vantage point.

Then Marshal Lewis rode by. He threw a covert look at the hotel, rode on. Brad arose and sauntered to the door. The fat man looked up from his chair. "I figured you'd give up."

Brad saw Lewis, well down the street, turn off onto the road that led to the Golden Eagle. Brad took a chair beside the fat man and hoisted his booted feet upon the rail. "In this heat, it pays to let others work."

Brad let the hot hours drag by, at ease on the shaded porch, dozing off at times, at others watching the torpid life moving along the street. Waco Mead came out, looked at Brad in surprise, then glanced at the fat man, and went out into the street. Brad watched him cross to the café and enter. A few moments later, Brad stood up, stretched as though he had nothing on his mind and also crossed to the café.

When he entered, Mary stood at Waco's table. She looked up when Brad entered, smiled, and then hurried to the kitchen.

Waco looked around with a scowl, motioned him to the table. "Just as well sit here as anywhere. With you around, she can't keep her mind on me."

Brad grinned, "Sure glad to know that."

"Oh, your turn now and mine later. You done your talking to those two people yet?"

"To one — and waiting. When the time's right, I'll talk to the other one."

"Mmm . . . hope this thing winds up soon. I keep thinking of Las Cruces. Time's wasting."

"Hang and rattle. You'll be heading east before you know it."

Just then Mary came out with Waco's order. She took Brad's, who noticed the way Waco covertly watched them as he ate, and scowled. Soon she served him and then merchants came in for the noon dinner. Brad kept watching the street through the window. He had just tackled his slab of dried apple pie when he saw Hank Lewis, obviously hot and irritable, ride by on his way to his office.

Brad did not hurry pie, nor coffee afterward. He paid Mary Alma with a smile that made Waco frown again, and then walked out. He went to the livery stable and, a few moments later, reappeared with his horse. He rode lazily down the street, aware that

Lewis had come to the door of his office to watch him. Brad rode on, unconcerned, and turned into the road leading to the Golden Eagle Mine. When the first adobe hid him from view of the main street, his hand touched the rifle stock beneath his leg and the Colt in his holster. Then he faced the barren mountains with a look as grim as their heat-blasted rocks.

He entered the first of the canyons, cast a sharp glance along the serrated rim. He expected no trouble until he reached the mine, even if there. Dean Harris would make no open move that would condemn him. Or, if he did, the man would make sure he held every advantage.

The silence of the mountains, the unmoving layers of heat seemed to support Brad's belief. He threaded the canyon, mile after mile, came out on the rim that overlooked the distant town. He drew rein to take in the faint breeze that blew out here, even though it seemed to come directly off hell's own fires. Everything below him, as far as he could see, shimmered in heat, waves of it ghosting up and down to the far horizon.

He finally turned the horse and headed toward the next canyon mouth. He approached within a few yards of it when he heard a faint sound, echoing down to him from the cleft. Brad instantly drew rein. At that moment, a rider burst out of the canyon, pulled in his horse to a sliding halt.

Brad had a glimpse of a dark, hawklike face with startling blue eyes and bright red hair. Face and slender body were Mexican, even the clothing and the large cruel spurs, the sombrero. But eyes and hair were Irish.

The impressions barely registered when the man whirled about and his hand slashed to his gun. It blurred up with amazing speed. Brad moved a split second later, throwing himself to one side as his fingers taloned to his holster. Both men moved too fast for accurate shooting. Brad felt the whip of the bullet by his head as his own wrist twisted, finger tightened, and the Colt bucked against his palm.

The man raced now into the mouth of the canyon, twisting about in the saddle, Colt spitting flame. Brad fired again, saw a slight jerk in the man's voluminous shirt sleeve. Then he vanished into the canyon, and the racing hoofs boomed and echoed.

Brad spurred hard and the bay jumped forward in pursuit. Dark face, blue eyes, and red hair — it could only be Juan Cochran. Brad leaned forward over the horse's head, spurs raking. The booming sound of flight filled the canyon.

# Chapter Sixteen

Brad raced down the torturous twists of the canyon, never quite getting sight of his quarry. Whip of wind, echoes of his own swift passage, made thunder in his ears. At each turn, he hoped to get Juan Cochran in his gunsight; but each sharp turn revealed only a short empty stretch of narrow canyon, broken here and there by deep clefts. Brad, lips peeled back from his teeth, urged the bay on.

Suddenly, and without warning he burst onto the wide plateau where the mine buildings stood. There was no sign of fleeing outlaw, and the buildings, barren ground, rock walls beyond seemed undisturbed by human fury.

Brad drew rein, the bay coming to a sliding, dust-raising halt. He looked back, realizing Cochran must have cut off into one of those narrow side canyons. Brad reined the horse about, and then recognized the futility of it. Cochran would know the maze of cuts, draws, and canyon as Brad knew the shape and look of his hand. He made a distasteful move of the lips and turned once again to the mine.

He heard the rumble of the mill and, as he rode forward, workers pushed a loaded ore cart out of the stope. They rolled it out of sight and, shortly, Brad heard a rolling rumble as the ore was dumped preparatory to curshing and reduction. He rode straight for the office shack.

He pulled in and dismounted. As he looped reins around the rack, he saw that men watched him from the mine entrance and some of the buildings. Dark faces reflected suspicion and a half-hidden hate rather than the fear they were supposed to show to lawmen. As Brad, horse securely tied, turned to the office, the door opened and Dean Harris stood framed.

It seemed to Brad the man's smile was somewhat forced but Harris spoke with easy surprise. "Well, Ranger! Didn't expect you back. I heard you'd ridden north for good."

"Rode north, all right, but not for good."

Harris descended the steps. "Come to the house. Maybe a couple degrees less hot over there, and there's something to drink. I reckon you'd accept one?"

Ruefully admitting to himself that the room was the most comfortable place in the whole area, Brad dropped into a chair a few moments later. Harris disappeared for a moment or two and reappeared with whisky and glasses. He poured for Brad, then his own, and sat down, lifting his glass. "To cooler days."

Brad smiled briefly, drank the toast. Harris sighed, stretching out his booted legs before him. "I'm glad you rode up, in a way. I've been fighting myself for an hour to leave that sweat-box office. A visitor makes a good excuse."

"Seen or heard from Juan Cochran lately?" Brad shot the question.

Harris replied easily, "That *bandido* won't be fool enough to show up here of all places! He robbed us, remember?"

"I remember . . . but I just had a brush with him."

Harris' stunned surprise was real enough. He jerked upright, eyes starting, body electrified. He caught his voice. "Juan! A brush!" He swallowed slightly. "You — arrested him? . . . or he's dead?"

"Neither. Chased him this way but he got away."

Harris jumped up. "We'll go after him! I'll get some of the boys!"

Brad shook his head. "He's far-yonder by now. Besides, I thought your Mexicans are afraid of him."

Harris sank back into the chair, made an exasperated motion with his hand. He emptied his glass in a single gulp. "You're right. If they even saw his dust, they'd cut and run. But it sure surprises me to know Cochran would dare come up this way."

"I thought he'd come from here, considering the canyon and the direction he rode."

"He'd know better!" Dean frowned, poured again for himself. "Come to think of it, what brings you?"

"Didn't Hank Lewis tell you I've been in Cochise Springs?"

"Hank? Where would I see him? I haven't been in Piedra Mala. He's not been up here."

"I thought he might." Brad did not press the point. It was enough to know that Harris lied.

"Nothing to bring him, now you're here. What took you to Cochise Springs?"

"Hunch, I reckon." Brad smiled easily. "A lawman goes a lot on hunch when nothing adds up."

"Well, it added up here! We were robbed. That's it."

"Not quite. Did Orin go up there regular?"

Harris seemed to collect his thoughts, but Brad sensed something more. "I never paid much attention to what Orin did when he wasn't at work. I never heard that he did, but that doesn't mean I know — one way or the other."

"And Callita? I hear some in Piedra Mala were surprised about that."

"Like I said, a man fools around the wrong places, he can get a knife down there — and Orin did."

"It's the fooling around down there — with the woman."

"Well, that surprised me, too." Harris frowned as though slightly puzzled. "But what has Orin's killing down there to do with you? That'd be a Rurale business."

"By the way, do you know any of the Rurales?"

"I've seen 'em now and then — I think a patrol works the border out of Callita. But I don't know them."

"Good lawmen — some of the best. They follow up any lead or tip." Brad paused a second but Harris seemed uninterested. Brad continued, "Funny thing in Cochise Springs — Orin changed hair and eye color between here and there."

"What!" Harris eyed Brad, not quite achieving honest surprise. "Now what does that mean?"

"I wish I knew, exactly. By the way, is there some small independent diggings around Piedra Mala?"

"There may be. I'm too busy with Golden Eagle to worry about dollar-a-day operations." Harris leaned forward. "Just why all these questions, friend? You're called in to catch an outlaw, and you seem to be doing everything else but that."

Brad arose. "Like I said, hunch about things that made me curious. You're right about my job down here. I'm still looking for the Golden Eagle robber — or robbers."

Harris' eyes flicked slightly, steadied. "Yes, more'n one — all that Cochran band. Sorry I can't help you much. This business about Orin — I don't know what to make of it."

"Well, I had the ride up — and I was almost lucky enough to nail Cochran. Maybe next time. Thanks, anyhow."

Harris became at ease again, and suddenly. "Anything I can do! How about another drink?"

Brad refused and Harris walked with him to his horse. The manager waved an apparently friendly good-bye when Brad reined around, and he walked directly to the office and inside. Brad again noticed watchful eyes from the buildings as he rode back to the canyon.

He rode slowly along, glancing at each side crevice. Most of them were too narrow for a horse, but finally he saw one wide enough. He looked down at the ground, saw the faint mark of a hoof. He rode on, after pausing a long moment.

He suddenly felt that he was watched. He twisted around in the saddle, but the canyon behind him was empty and the rims above revealed nothing. At last he rode on, the feeling still strong with him.

After he had disappeared around a turn, a man slowly straightened from the crevice wall against which he had flattened himself. Blue eyes in a dark face glittered angrily, and he made the typical gesture of snapping thumbnail from the teeth, then cursed. He faded back into the crevice, walked a distance to where it widened, and his horse waited. He mounted, rode out by a wider, different way into the main canyon. He turned toward the Golden Eagle.

He did not pause as he emerged from the canyon and boldly rode toward the office. His harsh glance swept over the few workers, who continued their labors without pause. Harris threw open the office door and made a fierce gesture for Cochran to hurry inside. The outlaw merely grinned stubbornly and continued his slow way to the hitchrack, took his time dismounting and tying his horse.

Harris had worriedly watched the far mouth of the canyon while the outlaw approached. As Cochran came up the steps with a measured, harsh stride, Harris snapped, "Are you asking for trouble!"

"No more than I have."

"Then get inside!"

Cochran smiled unpleasantly, paused on the top step. "Is it your neck, *amigo,* that will stretch or mine?"

Harris flushed, Cochran's grin grew wider, and he stepped inside. Harris closed the door. Cochran moved through the barrier swing gate and on to Harris' office. The manager spoke to the Mexican clerk who had looked around in mild curiosity.

"Stay by the window. If you see the Ranger in the canyon mouth, tell us."

He then went into his office and closed the door. Cochran stood by the small, open window, and he swung around when he heard Harris behind him. "That Ranger is too dangerous."

The manager dropped in his chair behind his desk. "Sit down, Juan. Between Hank, you, and Nolan, I'm getting a case of nerves."

Cochran turned to a chair, eased into it, adjusting his holstered Colt to the protruding chair arm. "Eh! *you* have nerves! We came face to face in the canyon mouth."

"I heard," Harris sighed. "And he asked if you were here."

Cochran pulled his loose shirtsleeve around, showed a small jagged tear. "His bullet — that close."

"Too bad you didn't kill him."

"I tried, *amigo,* I tried!" Cochran's dark face set in harsh lines. "What else did he ask?"

Harris made a helpless gesture. "You heard what he told Hank. Nolan caught onto a hell of a lot in Cochise Springs. He wants to know about Orin, about who brings gold to Wells Fargo, what other mines are down here."

"Too many questions — many too many. It would have been best to have kept the sheriff down here. This one, he finds trails, and everyone of them leads back right here."

"We have to get rid of him!" Harris burst out.

"I knew that from the time I heard he had ridden in," Cochran answered tightly. "If Louis Cardonez had not been a fool, it would have happened."

"Then you have to try again."

Cochran quietly and grimly contemplated Harris, who grew restive under the steady gaze. Finally Cochran sighed. "Let us look at things as they are, *amigo*. You tried to buy the Ranger off. That did not work. Louis tried to kill him, but Louis is dead — not him. You and Hank, you watch, and when he rides into Mexico where he does not belong, you set a trap for him with the Rurales."

Cochran leaned forward, his thumb jabbing at his own chest. "It nearly works, eh? But now I have the Rurales so close that I must come north of the border! But our Ranger is not in a jail down there. He is here. There are guns south, guns north."

Harris ventured, "You've lived that way a long time."

Cochran nodded. "And I could take care of myself because I worked alone. But now — Señor Lewis becomes frightened. You are having nerves, eh? What is more dangerous than a scared man? and what more than to have two of them as your partners?"

Harris slowly straightened, face paling a little. "What are you driving at?"

Cochran chuckled and dropped back. "See! You are more scared. You wonder what I will do — maybe about you?"

"No, Juan," Harris answered hastily, "I know you can be trusted the whole way. I wouldn't have gone into this deal if I hadn't thought it."

Cochran's long, dark finger lifted, cutting Harris short. "But we do not talk about me. We talk about you. Nerves, *amigo.* Zzzng! they snap — and who can say what happens, eh?"

"You know me better —"

"I know I fake a robbery of this mine for you. I take little gold but I am blamed for it. You pay me to cover what you and Lewis have stolen through the years. So you do not fear jail any more — except — Señor Lewis, Señor Orin, and I know the truth. I have shut Orin up. Now a Ranger comes. How am I to know that you won't have me killed?"

Harris jerked to his feet, really frightened with this train of thought. "For God's sake, Juan! You're loco!"

"Prove I'm not."

"How?"

"Kill the Ranger, or have him killed. It is easy enough for you to arrange it."

Harris stared, aghast, swallowed, and moistened dry lips. "Me? But you have the men!"

"I have them. But think, *amigo.*" He

pulled a worn, dull coin from his pocket. "I bet this against a pile of gold not a Mexican can now get close to the Ranger, or his friend. You have forgotten that one, eh? The one who acts like a lawman without a badge? On sight, the Ranger would try to kill me — and so would the other one. But he asks questions. He looks for me. I ride south, there are the Rurales. No, you are left."

"But — but — how can I!"

"You have gold. Use it. Buy a killer — or do it yourself. Maybe Señor Lewis will help. After all, he can be in trouble, too."

"No one would go up against Nolan —"

"And that other one, Señor Mead. No one? A rifle at a distance, a Colt slug through an open window, a knife in a dark passage. There are ways."

Harris leaned forward for support, his rigid arms bracing the desk top, his face white. "You're asking too much! I don't know how to go about it. I don't have the —"

"Guts for it?" Cochran stood up, dark face contemptuous. "Then let me help you, *amigo.* Orin is murdered, and you ordered it. If I am captured, I shall say so. If I am killed, Gregorio will say so for me. Under gringo law, you are a murderer, too, for you planned and ordered it. So you will hang. You will kick very hard while you die slowly. You like that, eh?"

Harris looked ill, haggard. Cochran walked to the door. "Does that help? Can you do it now?"

Harris only stared in a fog of horror and fear. Cochran studied him a long moment, and his thin lips slowly curled in open scorn. He spat on the floor, a deliberate gesture. "You make me have shame that my father was gringo. But still he had boldness, that one. You!" The outlaw spat again.

"You don't understand —"

"*Dios!* too much!"

Cochran opened the office door. He slammed it with such force that it shook the small building. Harris closed his eyes tightly and shuddered.

# Chapter Seventeen

Brad glanced out the hotel window as he talked to Waco in the latter's room. This window opened onto the rear of the hotel, and Brad saw the ugly shapes of scattered adobes and houses in the fast deepening twilight. Beyond, the mountains, high against the sky, seemed to fade back into darkness as the far-off stars grew brighter and blazed in blue velvet.

The room itself was unlighted, and in its corners the night seemed to draw strength and flow outward. Waco's figure, sprawled in a chair, lost definiteness as the shadows flowed by him and out into the darkening world. His voice seemed softened by the twilight and, paradoxically, all the more harsh because of it. "So you figure they'll move?"

"They have to." Brad sighed softly, thinking how false the peace of the evening. He could dimly hear soft sounds from the street, once a lift of deep laughter, but he felt a current of tension beneath it all.

Waco stirred, bringing Brad's thoughts back to the room and the pressing moment. Waco asked, "How do you figure it'll break?"

"Juan Cochran will have to show his hand, make some move against me. I think we can use him to catch himself."

"Now that's a neat trick if it can be done."

"I'm the target," Brad said soberly. "I'm the one who's been to Cochise Springs. I roweled Lewis and Harris. I'm the one to be shut up. So, I'll be in plain sight for them."

"Invite a slug!"

"In a way. Depends on you. While they gun for me, they won't be looking for you. That gives you a chance to move in while Juan Cochran has eyes only for me."

Waco said, "I can't see you running that risk alone."

"With your savvy and gunspeed, I don't think it's too much of a risk. Besides, I have a Colt, too, and can use it. Between us, we down or capture Cochran. The rest falls into place. We both ride out of Piedra Mala richer than we rode in."

Waco said nothing for a long moment, and then his voice came in heavy surrender.

"Okay. I don't like it, but it makes sense. When do we start this cat and mouse business?"

"Nothing like right now. Cochran's close and he's likely to make his move at night. I'll stay hitched five minutes after you leave the room. Then I'll go out on the street. Stay close but out of sight, and watch everything."

Waco slowly arose. Brad now could hardly see him but sensed his movement to the door. It opened, indicated by no more than a stir of warm air. Waco's voice came out of the darkness. "It'll take both of us watching, remember that. You're doing more than I'd have nerve to do."

"Not if you were in my shoes. Give you five minutes."

The door closed. Brad stood up and walked to the window, looking blankly out into the night. Maybe it was a crazy thing to do, he thought, and then he grinned crookedly, wondering how much of a risk Mary Alma would count him now. But it was for her — and this would be the last. After this, a different life. And, he hoped, with her. He straightened then, checked his Colt in the darkness, slid it in the holster, and turned to the door.

When he came out on the street, Waco was

not in sight. Night had now descended, slightly lessened by a sliver of moon above and the hot, golden bars of light the lamps from stores and saloons cast into the street. He saw three horses at the saloon hitchrack. A man came out of a store, moved along the far walk, and then was gone. Brad felt a touch of chill along his spine, but he rubbed his hand across his mouth and boldly descended the hotel steps.

He went to the saloon. Bright, reassuring lamplight flooded him as he pushed through the batwings. A second later, he thought of a bushwhacker lurking in the dark with him a full target. He dismissed that with a picture of Waco, somewhere behind him, and walked boldly to the bar.

"Oh, Nolan!"

He turned, instinctively tense. He saw Dean Harris alone at one of the tables. The man motioned him over. Brad's eyes cut to the other men in the room, a dozen at the bar, a few at the tables. None of them looked either suspicious or interested, and Brad came up to Harris,

"Sit down. Have a drink."

Brad pulled out the chair and Harris signaled the bartender, called, "Bring a bottle this time, along with the glass."

Brad said, "That's a lot of drinks for one

evening, even if I could stay."

"Well, maybe we'll find something to drink to."

Harris looked toward the bar, momentarily cutting off conversation. Under the glow of the overhead light, Brad noticed the drawn look about the man's eyes, the downward pull at the corner of the lips that gave the impression Harris deliberately held them firm by an act of will. This apparent casual meeting could be the setting of a trap, Brad knew, and he eased about in the chair to clear his Colt for a swift draw. The bartender plunked bottle and glass on the table and Harris poured the drinks.

He lifted his glass, "Here's to the wind-up of Juan Cochran."

"Amen to that!" Brad downed the drink. He then asked, "I figured you didn't want it tied up."

"But I do. Maybe a little differently, but still over and done with." Harris shot a glance about the room and leaned forward slightly. "Do you reckon you could forget being a Ranger — say 'til we have this talk?"

"Should I?"

"I think so. How about it?"

Brad nodded slightly toward the bottle. "A man accepts another's hospitality, the least he can do is listen."

Harris smiled and Brad noticed the momentary relief in it. Then the manager sobered. "When you first came, I told you how I felt about this whole business. The Company can recover, and there's more than enough gold ore to make up for what Juan took. A sheriff upset my men bad enough, but a Ranger . . . !"

"None of 'em run when I rode up the other day."

"Not that we noticed. But when I checked after you left, I found the mine had practically shut down. That's the sort of thing I want to end." Harris wiggled eagerly forward in his chair. "I know the Company will back me in getting into production. How much they pay for it, is something else. I made an offer the other day that I knew would be okayed. But it wasn't enough, I see."

"Not exactly. It was the idea of just riding off from a case."

Harris made a gesture of understanding and dismissal. "Sure, I can understand. But that's not doing me or the Company much good. I'm catching hell because production reports are down. Not my fault, but the men 'way off there in Chicago can't understand that. So, I'm willing to dip in my own pockets to keep my record and reputation as a mining manager bright and shining. I figure to move on to better jobs, sooner or later, and a black mark here won't help me."

Brad said nothing, but his eyes probed questions. Harris spread his hands palm up on the table. "What's it worth to you to report Juan Cochran has ridden deep into Mexico and won't be back?"

"Why should I?"

"Because he has! I just heard it. And your office can report it to the Rurales. It's all they can do, anyhow."

"It's just your word for it."

"Like I asked, how much is it worth to take my word?"

"How much is it worth to you?"

Again Brad detected faint relief touch the harried eyes, and then it was gone. Harris dropped back, pulled at his lip, and seemed to consider the question. He asked, abruptly, "You'd ride out come morning and report Juan gone for good?"

"Is that part of the deal?" When Harris nodded, Brad said, "But I haven't heard how much it's worth."

Harris said in a low, even voice, "Five thousand dollars — paid in gold dust right tonight."

Brad blinked. He couldn't help it. This was more than twice what Waco had offered and there was no risk. The case would close with his report and, with that report, his resignation. It was so simple, so easy.

Harris pushed, "How about it? A man don't often come on a windfall like that."

Brad had vivid, swift pictures of Mary Alma, a ranch somewhere, and with this amount of money, a far better chance of making it go. He saw Waco Mead, but money talked to Waco, too, and the man would understand. Here was raw, harsh decision right before Brad — here and now.

He could not help the slight contraction of his throat. He hastily arose. Instantly, fear swept over Harris' face, but he erased it in a second. Brad was hardly aware of it. "I . . . I have to think about it. I'll tell you."

"When? There's no time to waste. This is take it or leave it."

"Will less'n an hour make a difference?"

Harris hesitated, then shook his head. "I guess not. But why can't you tell me now!"

Brad shook his head and turned away. Harris called, "Wait!" He swallowed when Brad turned back. His eyes suddenly looked enormous, and Brad sensed a coiling horror and fear far back in them. He caught his voice. "This is important — to me. I wish I could tell you how important. You could be making the biggest mistake of your life if you turned it down. You could be —"

His voice cut off and his eyes closed tightly. He made a half-blind gesture. "Think it over but, for God's sake, know how important it is."

Brad stared at him, then wheeled and strode toward the batwings. He stepped out into the dark street and paused, looking about for Waco. But the bounty hunter kept hidden and Brad felt relief, a guilty one. He saw the light in Mary's café and turned in that direction, walking slowly.

Each step seemed filled with a hundred thoughts, fighting one another, clamoring for attention. *Five thousand!* one whispered, *It's grubstake!* Another intruded, *And what are you selling for it? It's soon spent, no matter what on, but you'll owe a mortgage on self-respect.* Another clamored in his head, *If you had this, Joanie wouldn't have turned you down. Without it, where do you think you'll stand with Mary Alma?* Yet another cut in, *What's a man worth after he's sold himself down the river? Who'll trust you? Will you trust yourself?* The first one derided, *Fine talk! but what does it buy! What does it lose!*

Brad found himself pushing open the door of the café. The tinkle of the bell, a small sound, sent the clamorous thoughts scampering, and he suddenly saw everything crystal and cold clear — himself, the table filled room, Mary at the far doorway. He also saw, equally clearly, that all arguments were in. He felt suddenly split — Brad Nolan awaiting decision and Brad Nolan who would hand that decision down, like a judge from a bench.

Mary advanced. "Brad! You had supper an hour ago! You can't be hungry."

"Coffee — and you, too. Please."

She looked strangely at him, then disappeared into the kitchen to return in a moment with two steaming mugs. She placed them on a table where Brad had seated himself. She went to the front door, turned the lock and pulled down the wide blinds, then returned to the table. "I was about to close, anyhow, so now we won't be interrupted."

He gave her a fleeting smile, sipped at his coffee, sought vainly to find some way to start. Mary toyed with her cup, a slight frown forming. "You've something very much on your mind."

He nodded, plunged. "Maybe I'm going to make a fool of myself, Mary. We've known one another a short time but . . . well, I've never before met a woman I wanted to marry."

"Brad!" Her eyes flew wide.

He hurried on. "I have to say it, tonight. I have to know how you feel."

"But — but —" Her lips formed an *O* as a thought struck her, "You're leaving Piedra Mala?"

"Soon. Look, I'm a Ranger, a lawman. I'm working at a job that has risk every day, sometimes every minute. Now, I know you don't want a man doing work like that. But . . . suppose I took off my badge?"

"Do you want to?" she asked slowly.

"For you. I've been thinking about it. Suppose I'd be able to say I'm going to start a ranch somewhere up north?"

"Do you want to do that, or is it for me?"

He dropped back in his chair. "Any man would want a life like that, with a woman like you. I'm tired of chasing up dim trails for just wages. Now, I have a chance to make the change."

He waited. Mary looked at the table and her coffee cup made aimless tracery. He could see only the soft, thoughtful purse of her lips, and he found himself waiting with as much tension as he would a meeting with Juan Cochran. He started to speak, changed his mind.

"I hear," Mary started abruptly, "no nice woman ever tells a man how she thinks about him. But — I have to say it. The first time you walked in the door, I knew you were something special. I didn't, and I don't, like the badge. I lost one husband in a dangerous job."

"But —"

"Let me finish, Brad. I don't know why tonight's so important for you, but let's say I'm not so sure I was completely right. If a man's fitted for his job and proud of it, then a woman has no right to take him away from it. She can either look to the man or look to the job, and make her own decision. I thought I'd look to the job. Now — it doesn't matter, though I would rather not lose a second husband to some outlaw's bullet. But I've got my choice, haven't I?"

"I said I could take off the badge. I have the chance."

She sighed and then smiled. "I'll not make the decision for you. It's not important. I don't think a man afraid to take chances because of a woman would make much of a husband in the long run. After a while, neither he nor the woman could be very proud of that kind of life."

Brad studied her for a long, long moment. He knew her dreams of security and a chance at a richer life. He had the chance to give it — his thoughts suddenly became clear and sharp. No, he didn't have the chance. He knew himself better than that. First, his pride in himself, his belief in himself; second, the oath he had taken when the badge was pinned on him, the trust that men had in him — all of this confirmed by what Mary had just said. He realized that, subconsciously, he had made his decision as he walked into this room.

Then his eyes lighted and his face glowed. The woman across the table was not a Joanie. She had also come to a decision. He reached across the table and took her hand. Her head jerked up, in a glowing, silent question.

"Then, you'll marry a Ranger?"

She nodded, caught her voice, "I'll marry Brad Nolan. He happens to be a Ranger."

He stood up so suddenly that his chair tipped over and crashed against the floor. Still holding her hand, he came toward her.

Gunshots, seemingly just outside the window, thundered and rocked the building. Brad heard a muffled cry. He and Mary stood frozen, half in each other's arms.

Then Brad whipped around and ran to the door.

# Chapter Eighteen

When the door resisted his tug, Brad remembered it was locked. Mary reached over his arm and turned the bolt. He blocked her way. "Stay back. A stray slug won't know you're a woman."

As he lunged into the street, he snatched the Colt from its holster. Two shots in quick succession brought him twisting around to the livery stable. He saw the dark silhouette of a man on the ground, clearly outlined in the stable's hanging lantern. He saw another lying just within the doorway, and then heard the fading pound of hoofs somewhere in the darkness beyond the light.

Brad, gun drawn, raced to the two fallen figures. He reached the first, bent down, one eye kept on the other in the stable doors. He glanced at the man beside him, first saw red hair and then Waco's pale face, eyes closed. An ugly stain spread from shoulder down over his chest. Brad felt a surge of fear as he touched the man. Waco's eyes fluttered open and he tried to sit up. He could no more than lift his head for a second before it dropped back.

"Juan?" he whispered. "Did he get away?"

"Cochran!" Brad whirled about and in two strides looked down at the man in the stable doorway. He saw Hank Lewis, dark face slack, a smear of blood along his skull above one ear. Brad felt for heart, heard it beating. He jumped back to Waco.

"No, it's Lewis. You gunned down the marshal."

"He was — with Cochran. Had a glimpse — left you to get Cochran. Caught him here — ready to ride out. Didn't see Lewis . . . until . . . threw down on me. I tried . . . get him. Then. . . ."

Waco's voice faded out and his eyes closed. Brad became aware that many men had come up and formed a silent, stunned, and curious ring about him. As Brad looked up, Mary pushed through the crowd. He saw the relief flooding her face as she looked at him, and then heard her gasp as she recognized Waco.

"Can you take care of him?" Brad asked sharply. "Shoulder wound."

She nodded and Brad straightened, the authority of the Rangers ringing in his voice. His stabbing finger indicated men at random. "You — you — you! Take this man where she tells you. Get a doctor."

"In Piedra Mala!" a derisive voice asked.

"Then you! — ride to the nearest one north or south of the border."

Men moved swiftly. They picked Waco up on an improvised stretcher made of coats and poles. Brad saw them move off with Waco, Mary following, telling Brad she'd nurse Waco at her house.

Brad then turned to Hank Lewis. The marshal remained unconscious where he had fallen. Brad saw his gun lying just within the doorway and scooped it up. He called on some more men to help him take Lewis to his office. Brad had the man stretched out on a bunk in one of his own cells, called for a lantern. He then carefully wiped the blood from the head wound.

He looked up and around. "A crease and nothing more. I can take care of him." The men did not move, and Brad's voice snapped, "That's it. Leave us alone. That's an order!"

They scowled, shuffled their feet, and then, under Brad's blazing stare, left the cell and the building. Brad followed them, closed and barred the front door, then returned to the cell, picking up the ring of keys on the way. He stood just within the barred door, studying the man sprawled on the bunk. After a moment, Brad stepped to him, unpinned the marshal's badge from the dark shirt, checked his pockets, roughly rolling the man over.

He had just confiscated a heavy Barlow knife when Lewis moaned, threw an arm out wide. Brad straightened, stepped back to the door. A moment later the marshal's eyes fluttered open, looked blankly at nothing, and then abruptly focused.

Lewis suddenly swung his legs from the bunk, and then fell back, grabbing his head. He looked up again, saw Brad, then the barred window, the door that Brad blocked. "How did I get here?"

"I had you carried in."

Lewis grimaced in pain, regained his voice. "Thanks for that favor, anyhow."

"No favor. A cell's where you belong anyhow."

The marshal looked up again, spoke through obvious nausea and a splitting headache. "Now what does that mean? This is my jail."

"Let's say it was. Now you're rooming here."

"Look, I don't feel like jokes! How about that gun-crazy saddlebum who threw down on me? Did I get him?"

"You'll wish you had," Brad said coldly. "That saddlebum, as you call him, teamed up with me to get Juan Cochran. He saw you helping an outlaw escape."

"That's a lie," Lewis shouted and then dropped back in pain.

Brad let the spasm pass. "You'll get a chance to prove that — before a judge and jury. I've arrested you for aiding an outlaw, for attempted murder. If Mead dies, it will be murder all the way."

Lewis, despite the pain, sat up. "Now you're crazy!"

Brad stepped out into the corridor, closed the door, and turned the lock. "With what I know about you, Lewis, you can count on a passel of years in Yuma, if Mead lives. I know you're the one who took gold to Cochise Springs, gold from the mine up there. That ties you in to Dean Harris, who stole the gold, and then had Cochran pull a fake robbery to cover it. I might even tie you into the killing of Orin below the border."

Brad paused a second. "And think this over. If Mead dies, you killed him. That's murder and, with all the rest, you'll hang. You can bet on it."

He turned and took a stride down the corridor when Lewis' sick voice checked him.

"Ranger!"

"Yes?"

Lewis looked about the cell, at Brad, and then shuddered. He moistened his lips. "What . . . what happens if I . . . well, sort of help you?"

"I don't need help. I think I can get the witnesses here and in Cochise Springs to prove what I know."

"But . . . if I made it so you wouldn't need to find witnesses?"

"Turn state's evidence?" Lewis swallowed deeply, shuddered again, and nodded. "In that case, Lewis, there'd be some leniency. I can't promise anything, but I'd do what I can."

"Then —" Lewis took a deep breath, "— listen. . . ."

When Brad left the jail, he had a full confession. He made a short trip to the hotel, returned with the fat man. He put a shotgun in the pudgy hands, indicated the rifle rack. "If anyone comes in, shoot first and question later. Savvy?"

"But I —"

"You're deputized," Brad snapped. "As soon as I can find some honest men, I'll send them to take your place."

He left the fat man seated on the edge of the chair behind the desk, shotgun lying across it, twin muzzles pointed toward the door. Brad took the keys himself. He strode out into the street and saw the knot of curious men. His eyes swept over them on the far chance he'd see Dean Harris and make that arrest, too. But the mine manager was not in sight, and Brad wondered if he had also run across the border.

He strode on to Mary's home, knocked on the door. She instantly opened it and indicated a hallway, down which lamplight streamed. "He's in there. The men undressed him and put him to bed."

"How is he?"

"I think — or hope — he'll live. It's a bad wound, but he has a lot of strength. Someone headed for Cochise Springs. The doctor ought to be here."

He made a questioning gesture toward the hallway and she nodded, followed him to the bedroom. The lamp had been turned low, and Waco lay on the bed beneath the covers, his face pale, a heavy sweat clearly showing on his forehead and around the lips. Brad noticed that the man's breathing seemed regular, though deep. He turned and walked softly from the room.

Back in the living room, Brad said, "He looks like he's sleeping. That'll be good."

She sighed wearily and dropped into a

chair. "Up until five minutes ago, he was delirious and threshing. I thought it would never end."

"It's passed now."

"But I worry it might return. I'll be glad when the doctor finally gets here." She looked up. "But what about you?"

"I locked Hank Lewis up in his own jail. He's under arrest." Brad indicated the bedroom. "Depends on what happens to Waco, what the final charge will be."

"The marshal! under arrest?"

He told her then of Hank Lewis' confession. She listened with stunned surprise as he revealed the scheme Dean Harris had worked with Juan Cochran to cover the steady drain of the mine's gold. Mary shook her head. "It's hard to believe!"

"But there it is. I not only have Lewis' word for it, but I made him go over it while I wrote it down, and then he signed it. Funny, when a crook thinks his own neck is endangered, he'll not wait a minute to throw the blame on all his partners. I've seen it time and again."

"I can understand Juan Cochran. But our own marshal — and Dean Harris!"

"He hinted at a bribe when I first rode in, Mary. I'm not surprised at what I found in Cochise Springs or what Lewis told me. A man like Harris fits the picture."

Brad looked around the small but pleasant room and then at Mary, lovely in the lamplight despite the subtle touch of weariness about her mouth and eyes.

Impulse, and the moment, made Brad speak. "This whole business down here has been strange. When I met Waco, he made a deal with me about splitting the reward if I'd help him catch Cochran."

"But what's wrong with that? It's your job."

"That's what I told myself — and just about then I figured I'd wasted my time with the Rangers — for low wages, a word of thanks, and that's all. Waco told me that. So, I agreed — and began to doubt myself from that minute."

He leaned forward, elbows on knees, looking earnestly at her. "Then Harris hinted at a bribe. You know, Waco's deal almost made me ready for Harris? Then, just tonight, Harris raised the ante. I was to ride out, report Cochran had escaped for good to Mexico. All I had to do was agree, ride out and I had five thousand dollars."

Mary gasped, then her eyes narrowed. "That's when you came to me at the restaurant?"

He nodded. "Now, Lewis has talked Harris right into jail. What do you figure I could get out of Dean Harris to keep my mouth shut?"

She was silent a moment, then asked, "Would you?"

"Yesterday I'd have thought it over. Not tonight. I want to ride out as clean as I left Tucson."

She moved half out of the chair, reached out, and touched his hand. "Brad? That's what I want for you."

He covered her hand with his own. "For a time, I didn't figure you'd look at any man who wore a badge and worked for just wages. . . . A woman I knew in Tucson — well, that's past — then Waco, and the way he talked."

"I know." She sank back. "I said he's been delirious. Money rules mostly with him, except when he's made a promise or deals with a friend. I listened to him, and I felt I heard some of the thoughts I've had since my husband died, coming out of Waco's lips. I didn't like the sound of them. A dollar buys a lot of things but then you come to realize it sells a lot of things — of more value than it buys."

They fell silent for a moment, and then Mary broke the interlude. "Harris, Lewis, and — in a lesser way — Waco! They're sort of the end of the money trail, aren't they?"

"I nearly rode it."

"I'm so glad you didn't! And even more glad you turned back on your own!"

He laughed. "Come to think of it, how come I lost my badge down in Mexico? Now a new one's coming, and it'll be clean!"

She caught the idea and her face lighted. Impulsively, she left her chair, crossed to him, and bent down to kiss him. His arms reached for her.

The crash of the window glass and Mary's sudden jerk came simultaneously. She had been half-whipped around, and Brad saw the ragged tear in the sleeve of her dress, her stunned look. He whipped out of the chair, a single stride taking him to the lamp on the table. His breath snuffed it out as his Colt jumped from the holster.

Mary's voice came from the darkness. "I'm really not hurt. Who was it?"

"I'll find out," Brad snapped and jumped to the door.

He opened it, flattened to one side, as gun flame lanced orange a short distance away. The slug slammed into the door frame as Brad's gun swung up. He placed shots to either side of the place where he had seen the flame. He heard a man's screaming yell and saw a shadow move, drop. He raced forward at a crouch, hearing a dull thrashing ahead.

He came upon the writhing man, saw a faint glitter of metal, and kicked a gun to one side. Suddenly, the man came to his feet, crouched, and lunged to escape. Brad slammed a slug just ahead of the figure and the man froze.

"Stand up!" Brad thundered, "and reach high."

He advanced slowly, gun leveled, hammer dogged back. He realized the figure held up only one arm. "Lift your other hand!"

"Can't. Something's broken."

Brad recognized the voice. "So you've turned to attempted murder and gunning down women, Harris?"

# Chapter Nineteen

Brad, with a curt word, ordered Harris back to the house. When they entered, Mary stepped back from the door into the room, shrinking from Harris, who would not meet her eyes. Brad's first concern was for her but she showed the jagged rip in her sleeve, a grazing wound that had hardly more than burned skin deep enough to bleed, and a bullet hole in the far wall.

Brad turned blazing eyes on Harris. "You meant the slug for me!"

The manager flinched away, still clutching his dangling arm. Only then, Brad saw the drip of blood from his fingers. He curtly ordered the man to shrug out of his coat, helping Harris with one hand while he kept his leveled gun in the other. Brad asked Mary to bring material for bandages, and she hurried to the back of the house.

Brad said tightly, "First you try to bribe me, and then try to kill me. Was I too close to the truth?"

Harris said nothing and Brad continued, "This murder would have done you no good. Hank Lewis has made a signed confession. With me dead or alive, you'd still stand trial. We know the deal you made with Cochran, and why. We know you ordered Orin's murder — and it wasn't over a woman. Did he try to blackmail you?"

Harris sat silent a moment, then shrugged. "Since you know the rest — no, he didn't. He found out we were using his name in Cochise Springs. I figured if something come up, the law would look for a man named Orin. He threatened to tell the sheriff right after Juan's raid. So. . . ."

Mary came into the room. Brad stood to one side while she doctored and bandaged the arm as best she could. Then he made Harris precede him to the door. Brad spoke over his shoulder to Mary. "I'm locking this one up, along with his friend. Can you handle Waco?"

"Yes, but what will you do?"

"Talk to our friend here a while."

He marched Harris to the jail, called to the fat man to unlock the door. He marched Harris inside and to a cell, the fat man following, eyes for once distinguishable in the rolls of flesh. Brad locked the cell door, waved the corpulent jailer down the corridor, and looked through the bars at Harris.

"It's over and done. Lewis is down the corridor. He'll keep you company until you come to trial. Juan Cochran's below the border, and it's too hot for him up here now. You might help yourself a little bit, like Lewis did when he confessed."

Harris made a pain-filled grunt. "How?"

"I'd like to bring Juan Cochran in. I figure he won't show up in Callita or that village because of the Rurales. It's as hot for him down there as it is here. So — where would he go?"

"Why should I know?"

"You'd know — in case you needed him in a hurry."

Harris merely turned painfully on the bunk, showing his back to Brad. After a moment, Brad said, "All right. I'll see the judge throws the book at you."

He moved away, but Harris checked him. "How do I know you can help with a judge and jury?"

"I can tell the judge if you worked with me or against me. A criminal who tries to make up in some way for what he did generally gets consideration. I won't promise anything, though. It's up to you."

Not long after, Brad came out on the

street, paused, hearing the fat man turn the door lock behind him. Brad stood a moment, looking south into darkness, recalling what had last happened down there. It could happen again, he knew. He turned his head, looking in the direction of Mary's home, seeing the jagged tear of the near-miss on her sleeve, Waco lying pale and slack on the bed. His jaw firmed.

He hitched at his gunbelt and turned to the hotel. He came out soon, rifle and scabbard in his hand and crossed to the livery stable. He led his horse from the stall and saddled with swift efficiency. Then he straightened, paused, knowing he again ran a risk of a bullet or a Mexican jail. But this time, there was a pressure, for Juan Cochran would not remain long in one place. He'd feel safe now, but tomorrow, or the next day, he'd move on and be lost to American justice. Brad swung into the saddle, turned the horse south, and rode out of town.

Nearing what he judged to be the international line, Brad drew rein. He placed Callita, the village, and what Harris had told him about the location of Juan's hideout, known only to Gregorio and none of the rest of his band of killers. Brad set his direction by the high clear stars and, satisfied, left the road. He could not run the chance of riding right into a Rurale patrol.

The dark hours and the miles passed. He knew that he had worked his way south of Callita and the village, each of them lying behind him to left and right. He judged the time and then, knowing he would need at least dawn light to locate the hideout, he dismounted, ground-tied the horse, and made himself as comfortable as he could.

He dozed fitfully, awakening now and then with a start to continued darkness. He'd doze off again. But the first faint suggestion of dawn found him wide awake. He walked about in small circles, working the stiffness out of muscles, and when he could at last see the faint shape of distance cactus, he swung into saddle again.

Now he headed due east, intent on hitting the main road from Callita south into the heart of Sonora. The sun had just appeared on the far edge of the horizon when he saw the broad swath through the desert that marked the road. He seemed to be alone in this immensity of arid land, and sighed with relief.

He drew rein and studied the lay of the country about him. He checked over what Harris had told him, looked northward and saw the low twin rounded shapes of hills, like a woman's breasts. The first landmark, he knew, and his lips set in grim satisfaction as he set the horse to them.

He reached them, rode parallel to the northern hillock. Now the main road lay a mile or more west, and he was safe from chance discovery from patrols or riders. Still he kept cautious attention divided between the distant road and the hills to his right, and his hand was never far from his Colt. He began to circle the second hillock, and now he slowed his horse, attention wholly on what lay ahead.

As he moved about the irregular curve, the vista beyond slowly expanded. He saw, at first, only a continuation of the arid, cactus and brush-studded country over which he had traveled. Then, as he moved on, he saw a grove of palo verdes, those lovely but scant desert trees. He caught a glint of water, and then saw a series of cattle pens in ill repair, some low adobes, roofs fallen in.

He drew rein, eyes narrowed as he studied the distant structures. He realized the pens had long since been abandoned and that he looked on a rancheria that had failed many years before. He lifted the reins and the horse moved forward, held in tight check. More of the vista opened and then Brad saw what had once been the main building.

At first glance, it also gave the impression of complete desertion, that nothing lived in it but the desert reptiles and rodents. Its once solid front door hung askew, and the narrow windows in the thick walls looked blind and empty.

But this, Brad knew from what Harris had said, was Juan Cochran's temporary refuge. Harris himself had been here on occasion. Brad then saw the trail leading to the southmost hillock and circling it toward the road. He discerned another leading south and eastward. The years since this rancho had been in operation would have obliterated those trails had they not been in occasional use.

Brad considered his approach, not daring to risk the fairly open space between himself and the ruined rancho. Before he could traverse even a quarter of the distance, he would be seen. Then, he saw that one circuitous route might give him the chance to drift in unseen. Off to the left, the slender trees, tangle of ancient pens, and some of the abandoned shacks made that section of the main house blind to approach in that direction. He turned back toward the curve of the hill and rode partially around it. Then he made a wide circle, far beyond sight of the rancho, and again drifted in.

When he came in sight of the rancho again, he nodded in grim satisfaction. This far out, at least, he could see only the trees, the distant pens. The house beyond was blocked from his sight and therefore, he would not be seen. He moved forward slowly.

Some distance out, he came upon a shallow depression, probably formed over the years by the rush of waters from the barren distant mountains when cloudbursts came. Brad breathed a sigh of thanks, rode down into it, and dismounted. Now, he could not see above the rounded rim of the arroyo. He ground-tied the horse, pulled rifle from its scabbard, and went ahead afoot.

Topping the rim, the main house was still hidden. He could get very close afoot where, riding a horse, he would have been instantly spotted. As he came closer, he had occasional glimpse of the house, but he reached the broken pens and then one of the decrepit shacks, without alarm. Now he saw, behind the house, a corral and rickety shelter under which stood a horse. Brad's eyes gleamed in pleasure. Juan had not fled!

But Brad could not reach him. He now could see the rear of the house. A solid door was closed, and the embrasured windows here looked threatening rather than blind.

He could see the trampled area about the door, leading to the horse shelter and corral. Rising sun glinted off a tin, and he saw rusted cans at the edge of the cleared space beyond the door.

Brad bit at his lip, then with impatient resignation, moved back into the interior of the shack to wait developments. Juan might come out and, if he did, Brad's assignment would be only a matter of getting his prisoner back across the line where an arrest would be official. But the solid door remained closed, and the one window Brad could see from his vantage point revealed nothing within the house. Brad hunkered down against the far wall in the corner. This was a time for patience.

The changing angle of sun across the doorway told of the slow passage of time. Heat increased, trapped in this small area, and Brad felt wrapped in it. Nothing stirred outside and, had it not been for the horse in the shelter, Brad would have believed the place devoid of life. He thought, grimly, Juan has to show himself sooner or later.

Suddenly, sometime in the early afternoon, he stiffened. He heard a distant call. He came to his feet, shaking the heat-drowze from brain and eyes. He heard a closer call, obviously from the front of the house. Brad waited and the minutes seemed to drag. Suddenly he heard voices, two men who talked as they approached the shack. Brad's gun leveled on the door, and he moved swiftly to be out of direct sight from the yard.

The voices grew louder, and Brad's thumb lifted up and over the hammer, ready to dog it back. Dull steps sounded just before the door, and he saw the shadow of two men momentarily projected on the floor of the shack by the beam of sunlight. Then they passed on. He heard a door slam. Silence.

He moved cautiously, looked out. A saddled horse now stood droop-headed before the house. Saddle and stirrups were ornate, and the bit was one of those cruel Spanish inventions. Brad edged back waiting developments. They seemed forever in coming but finally he heard sudden loud voices. He risked a swift glance, saw Juan Cochran and his lieutenant, Gregorio.

Gregorio wore one arm in a dirty sling, Brad saw before he flattened himself out of sight against the inner wall. He could not follow the swift Spanish of the two men, but did catch a word now and then. "Tonight!" was repeated several times. "Manuel," came clearly, then "Harris," followed by a curse. Suddenly a horse moved and

Brad saw its crooked silhouette passing the doorway. Sound faded and Brad again chanced a look outside. He caught a glimpse of Juan entering the house, and then the door closed. Brad, with an inward curse, knew that he must continue the wait until dark.

Finally the sun's shafts across the door became long and mellow, gradually faded. Brad stirred from his corner, checked his Colt, and moved so he could see the house. The door remained tightly closed but, as the light slowly faded, Brad knew this to be less of an obstacle. Day merged into a twilight with a reddish glow as the sun touched the far horizon. Suddenly the door opened and Juan stepped out.

Brad froze, but the outlaw did not look toward the shack. He moved beyond the doorway out of sight. Brad jumped to the entrance, saw Juan go to the shelter. He checked his horse, disappeared beyond the corner of the shack to reappear with a battered bucket of water for the animal. When the horse had finished, Juan carelessly dropped the bucket to one side. Fading sun glinted on the metal of the gun in his holster.

He slowly turned, eyes to the western sky. Brad eased out of the door, gun leveled.

"Lift 'em high, Juan."

The man jerked half around, caught himself. He stood rigid, and his arms slowly lifted. He was turned half away from Brad, who advanced slowly. Beyond Cochran, the horse looked at Brad with equine curiosity. Other than the lift of its head, Brad's slow step, there was no movement, hardly any sound. Brad reached out for the Colt in Juan's holster. The outlaw stood immobile.

Brad's finger tips touched the wooden grip. Juan suddenly exploded in action. He whirled about to the left, and his arm flailed back, catching Brad a glancing blow on the head. Brad's head snapped aside and his finger tightened on the trigger. The Colt bucked against his palm, and the bullet missed Juan by only a fraction of an inch.

Juan had continued his whirl, his right hand slashing down to the Colt Brad had just touched. It blurred upward as Brad's wrist twisted about, and his gun flamed again. The slug smashed into the outlaw's lifting weapon, smashing it from his fingers as the bullet whined high in a vicious ricochet. Juan's fingers splayed out, an automatic reflex from the paralyzing strike of the bullet. His gun whipped in a low arc far to one side.

Juan grabbed his right hand, face twisting

in pain. He froze when Brad's voice whipped at him. "Hold it!"

Juan's pain-filled eyes glittered hate and defeat. "You're lucky, *ladron.*"

"*You* were. I was shooting to kill. That slug went wild. The next one won't." Brad slowly straightened from his crouch. "I reckon we'll head north, Juan. Saddle up — and no wrong moves."

He kept his gun on the outlaw as Juan picked up the saddle at the end of the shelter, slapped it on his horse. He adjusted bit and bridle and then turned, dark face now inscrutable but the eyes alert. He waited for the slightest turn of luck, Brad knew. Brad made a slight gesture with his weapon. "Lead the horse out and walk it ahead of me."

On Brad's curt order, they walked toward the shallow swale. Purple shadows now began to creep across the barren land, and the shape of the twin hills began to fade into the landscape. They came into the swale, found Brad's horse. Brad ordered Juan to mount, cross his hands behind his back, after Brad pulled the steel, linked cuffs from his own saddlebag. He snapped them around Juan's wrists, and only then walked to his own horse and mounted.

They headed directly north, Brad taking

his direction from the bright evening star glittering over the darkening land. The palo verde trees and ancient pens faded swiftly behind them, and Brad felt an easing of tension. He ordered Juan to halt, dismounted, and took the coiled rope from his saddle. He fastened it on the cheek strap of Juan's horse, ran it back to his own, then remounted, and, giving slack, looped it around his saddle horn. Satisfied, he ordered Juan on ahead.

Soon they rode through the full night, over a mysterious dark land. Now and then, brush, cactus, or desert tree would loom out of the shadows, swiftly fade behind them. For a time, Brad watched the brooding night land behind, thinking of the chance of pursuit. Gregorio and Manuel had something to do tonight, and it might well be a meeting with Juan. But as time and the miles passed and there was no alarm or sound of pursuit, Brad dismissed the problem. The two outlaws could not possibly trail their missing leader until dawn.

Now and then Brad felt a slight tug on the rope as Juan's horse forged ahead a little faster than his own. But the check was always sufficient, and the steel bracelets around Juan's wrists behind his back prevented any chance of escape. There remained only the miles of Mexican desert to be traversed.

They seemed endless. Juan rode in surly silence, but Brad knew the man only waited for a last, slim chance to escape jail and the gallows north of the line. Deep in the night, Brad called a halt, let Juan dismount, and walked just behind him in erratic circles. The stiffness left their muscles, and Brad ordered the outlaw back to his horse.

The man remounted and, on order, placed his hands behind his back and Brad snapped the cuffs back in place. Then Juan finally spoke, "You are wealthy, Ranger?"

Brad laughed harshly. "Before you begin, you'd better know Harris tried a bribe. He's in jail, along with Lewis, waiting for you. Let's ride."

They moved on, Brad again setting the direction and now riding at an angle to hit the main road just above the border and below Piedra Mala. Only he and Juan moved in this sleeping land, and with each forward step, the end of the trail drew closer. This would end, Brad thought in thankfulness, without trouble in a matter of an hour or so.

He judged the distance and knew the invisible border must be close ahead and, just beyond, Piedra Mala and Mary. The mental picture of her warmed him and he began, lazily, to dream of the future. Now and then the rope between the horses would alternately tighten and slack off. They suddenly came on the road and Brad peered ahead hoping for a glimpse of a far-off light that would mark the town. The darkness was unbroken, however. The late hour, not long before dawn, would explain that. This was undoubtedly Arizona, and Sonora lay a short distance behind him.

He felt tension leave him. "Almost there, Juan, though that won't please you much."

He had spoken louder than he thought or the night stillness had magnified his voice. It seemed to vibrate out into the darkness. At that moment, a challenge sang out in a sharp Spanish voice. It was just ahead and a little to one side. Brad jerked erect in the saddle, alarm coursing through him.

Juan's yell split the silence as Brad sank spurs and, grabbing the lead rope, raced off to the left. The voice ahead yelled a command to halt, and then Brad heard the word "Rurales!"

He had stumbled on a patrol camped for the night at the border, waiting for smugglers or night riders like Juan and himself. Brad's lips peeled angrily back from his teeth. This close! and to be thwarted! Rurales posed as much a danger to him now as any of Juan's band. A gun flamed behind him, and the bullet sang dangerously close over his head. Brad raked spurs, glad that Juan could in no way check the flight.

He heard shouts behind him and, then the thundering roll of hoofs as the Rurales came on in pursuit. Guns flamed again, the bullets searching him out. He sensed that the Mexican lawmen fanned out in a ragged crescent behind him, one arm racing to prevent him crossing into Arizona. He dared not be caught this second time, especially with a prisoner illegally taken in defiance of treaty laws. His impulse was to return the fire, if only to check pursuit, but he knew the Rurales would only center in on him. He had to depend on speed and darkness.

Both horses raced through the night, going at such a speed that Juan dare not throw himself from the saddle. In fact, Brad had the fleeting thought, Juan faced the devil's choice. He no more dared be taken by Rurales than he dared be led across the border by Brad. Raking spurs urged continued speed from the horses and, in the darkness, Brad heard the continuing sounds of hot pursuit.

He angled to the right now, heading north,

hoping to ride beyond the point of the Rurales seeking to cut him off. Now neither pursued nor pursuers wasted lead in gunfire. The faint gray shape of the ground blurred by under pounding hoofs. To the left and south, the Rurale point riders began to angle in, intent on encircling and trapping. Brad's spurs raked again, and now he leaned out of the saddle and slapped coiled rope on Juan's horse.

He could hear only the rush of wind by his ears, the steady drumbeat of his horse's hoofs and those of Juan's. Now and then he sensed a brush whipping by. His horse strained forward, giving its might to the urge of the spurs. Suddenly guns slammed behind him. and Brad heard the whine of bullets. He heard Juan's horse squeal, sensed its stumble and falter, pulled in just as the animal collapsed, spilling Juan.

Brad jumped from the saddle, jerking rifle from scabbard, knowing now he had to make a stand against men of his own kind if not nationality. Perhaps rifle bullets would hold them at a distance until he could work Juan onto his own mount and make the safety of the border without being recognized. With the beat of hoofs no longer in his ears, Brad realized that pursuit had stopped. He heard vague movement far out, and aimless weaving back and forth, voices calling in disappointment to one another in staccato Spanish.

Brad slowly straightened, rifle still in his hand. He had made the border! Those Rurales would know it and so they had pulled in, helpless. Brad's breath eased slowly out of tight lungs and then he became aware of Juan's spitting curses on the ground nearby. Brad turned toward him, bent down, and jerked him to his feet. He loosened the rope from the dead horse, dropped it over Juan, and tightened it.

Holding an end of the rope, Brad swung into saddle. He spoke to Juan in quiet triumph. "Piedra Mala's just ahead somewhere, not so far you can't walk it. Head out."

In an uncertain half light from the eastern horizon, Brad saw the buildings just ahead a half hour or so later. Juan trudged ahead of him, manacled hands behind his back, shoulders bowed. They came into the main street. Nothing stirred in the sleeping town that looked uglier as the pale light strengthened. A lamp glowed in sickly yellow from the marshal's office, and Brad headed toward it.

After a moment, the fat man answered Brad's peremptory knock and low identification. The door swung back and the fat man's eyes bulged when he saw the prisoner. "Cochran!"

"No less," Brad answered in weary satisfaction. "Let's get him in a cell."

In a few moments, Brad and the fat man returned to the office, the cell and corridor doors tightly locked behind them. Brad dropped into a chair, suddenly feeling the racing miles, the day and the night behind him. He sighed, closed his eyes, and felt weariness wash over him. He fought it down, straightened with an effort.

The fat man watched him, mouth still open in surprise. "How did you get Cochran?"

"I got him, that's what counts — not how." Brad realized fatigue had roughened his voice. He softened it. "Give me a chance to rest and feed, and I'll tell you."

"Your room's waiting at the hotel, so far as I know." The man grunted. "I've had to let it go to hell since you shoved me in on this job."

"That'll soon be over." Brad swiped his hand over his face, feeling the stubble on jaw and chin, "Soon's we find someone we can trust to keep them safe."

He indicated the cells. The fat man yawned. "Will the sheriff do?"

Brad galvanized. "He's here!"

"Be here sometime today." He explained, "The gent who rode for the doctor found him, by luck, 'way this side of Cochise Springs. The doctor come on but sent the feller to Cochise where the sheriff just showed up. So, I reckon the law will ride in any time."

Brad sighed in relief, then another worry caught him. "The doctor's here?"

"Yup."

"Waco Mead?"

"Doc says he'll make it. Won't have much of a gun arm for a while but that'll pass."

Brad pulled himself from the chair, again bone weary and weakened by relief. "I'll hit that hotel bed, and then see Mary Alma when the town wakes up."

He turned but the fat man suddenly jerked open the desk drawer. "Clean forgot. Man rode in from Cochise Springs. Brought this for you."

He extended a small wrapped package. Brad, puzzled, snapped the string, tore off the brown paper to reveal a fiat box. He opened it and a bright Ranger badge glittered in the lamplight.

Unexpected thoughts raced through his mind, a succession of images — the badge on his breast again — Tucson and his report

— Mary Alma's face — her decision that he should do the job that suited him. It would make no difference. He saw them together in a house that existed somewhere in the future.

He lifted the badge from the box. "New badge?" the fat man asked, frowned. "What happened to the one you had?"

"Lost — and just as well. Might turn up some day and cause a little trouble." He saw the man's puzzled look. "Got kind of tarnished, or started to get that way. But now. . . ."

He pinned the badge to his shirt, pulled the cloth out to admire it. "Bright, ain't it?"

"Sure — but it's new."

"That's right," Brad answered. "Nothing's happened to this one . . . nor will."

He walked out the door, feeling the good weight of the metal on his breast. Behind him, the fat man stood in the office doorway, thick arm lifted to scratch his head.

In the east, the sky brightened in soft, bright colors as the new day slowly came over the horizon.

The employees of Thorndike Press hope you have enjoyed this Large Print book. All our Thorndike, Wheeler, and Kennebec Large Print titles are designed for easy reading, and all our books are made to last. Other Thorndike Press Large Print books are available at your library, through selected bookstores, or directly from us.

For information about titles, please call:
(800) 223-1244

or visit our Web site at:
http://gale.cengage.com/thorndike

To share your comments, please write:
Publisher
Thorndike Press
10 Water St., Suite 310
Waterville, ME 04901